Happy Last Halloween.

The drawing was crude, done in colored markers.

A big orange jack-o'-lantern filled the page. But instead of the open, jagged grin that most jack-o'-lanterns have, this one was frowning. An angry frown.

Lowering her gaze, Brenda saw that the frowning jack-o'-lantern rested in a puddle of bright red ink. Red drips rained down to the bottom of the page.

Blood? she wondered.

Is it resting in blood?

And then she saw the words scrawled in heavy black marker across the bottom:

HAPPY LAST HALLOWEEN.

Don't miss these other thrillers by R.L. Stine:

HALLOWEEN NIGHT II

R.L. STINE

SCHOLASTIC INC.
New York Toronto London Auckland Sydney

ISBN 0-590-47482-0

12 11 10 9 8 7 6 5 4 3 2 1   4 5 6 7 8 9/9

Printed in the U.S.A.   01

First Scholastic printing, September 1994

HALLOWEEN NIGHT
II

Chapter 1

Brenda Morgan tossed her long, copper-colored braid behind her shoulders. "Get out of my kitchen, Angela," she cried angrily.

Angela Bowen stood defiantly against the white kitchen counter, her hands pressed against her waist. Her dark eyes flashed angrily. "Not until we talk, Brenda," she replied coldly.

"Get out," Brenda snarled. "Get out of my house." She clenched her hands into tight fists at her sides.

Angela let out a scornful laugh. "You're such a jerk, Brenda. Really."

Balling and unballing her fists, Brenda moved out of the shaft of afternoon sunlight that beamed through the kitchen window. She took a menacing step toward her friend.

Angela's smile faded. The light seemed to dim in her brown eyes as she glared unblinkingly back at Brenda. "Did you really think you could go out with Larry and I wouldn't find out about it?"

Brenda's mouth dropped open in surprise. Her face turned bright pink, and the freckles on her nose and cheeks darkened. "Is *that* why you're here?"

The kitchen clock chimed, four soft rings. Four o'clock. Clouds rolled over the sun. The kitchen darkened suddenly, as if someone had clicked off a light.

Angela tapped her polished orange nails tensely against the kitchen counter. A sneer formed on her round face. "Don't act innocent, Brenda. I'm not stupid, you know."

Brenda let out an exasperated sigh. "Why don't you go talk to Larry, Angela? Why come to me? Why burst into my house — uninvited — and start accusing me?"

"Listen, Brenda — " Angela started, narrowing her eyes in growing rage. "Listen to me — !"

"No!" Brenda shouted shrilly. "No! Just go home! I mean it — get *out* of my house!" Her hand trembled as she pointed toward the kitchen door.

"What about the Halloween party?" Angela demanded, ignoring Brenda's cries.

"Huh?" Brenda stopped short.

"The Halloween party," Angela repeated, her mouth twisted in an angry sneer. "Is Larry taking you to the Halloween party or not?"

Brenda's cheeks darkened from pink to crimson. "I told you. Ask Larry."

Angela opened her mouth in an angry cry. Her dark eyes flared, and her hands shot forward as she leaped at Brenda in fury.

Brenda tried to duck away. But Angela had her hands around Brenda's throat before she could move.

"Let go — !" Brenda managed to choke out.

She swung her fist hard, sending a glancing blow to Angela's shoulder. Then Brenda struggled and twisted, grabbing Angela's wrists, prying them off her throat.

Crying and gasping loudly, they wrestled each other to the floor.

Angela drove her knee into Brenda's ribs. Brenda reached up to the top of Angela's head and grabbed her brown hair with both hands.

Sobbing, panting, her mouth open, her chest heaving, Angela pulled out of Brenda's grasp and shot to her feet.

Brenda rolled away.

She raised herself to her knees — and stared up at the knife.

The gleaming, white-bladed kitchen knife grasped so tightly in Angela's hand.

"Angela — put it down!" Brenda screamed in a quivering, high voice. "Put it down!"

Angela's eyes bulged wide. Beads of sweat glistened on her forehead.

"Angela — no! Put it down!" Brenda pleaded, still on her knees.

Angela didn't seem to hear her. "What about Larry?" Angela screeched. "What about Larry?"

"Let's talk! Please — let's talk!" Brenda pleaded, raising both hands as if they could shield her.

Angela struck quickly.

She pushed off from the kitchen counter, dove toward Brenda, swinging the fat blade of the kitchen knife down with a low groan of anger — and pleasure.

Chapter 2

Her hands still raised above her head, Brenda toppled helplessly onto her back.

The knife plunged down as if in slow motion.

She watched the gleaming blade inch down, down, down . . .

Until a frightened voice rose over her gasps. *"Hey — stop! Angela — what are you doing?"*

Angela glanced up, startled. Her arm relaxed. The knife blade hung suspended, six inches from Brenda's chest.

"What are you doing?" Randy, Brenda's ten-year-old brother, leaped onto Angela's back and tugged her arm back with both hands.

Still on her back, Brenda started to laugh.

As Randy tugged Angela's arm, the knife slid out, onto the floor. Angela spun around, laughing, and wrapped her arms around Randy's waist.

"You ruined it!" Brenda told her brother.

She sat up, shaking her head. "You ruined the whole scene!"

"Huh?" Randy gaped at her. He squirmed free from Angela's hug. He saw that both girls were laughing. "What did I ruin? What's so funny?"

Traci Warner, Brenda's best friend, stepped out from behind the kitchen table. She lowered the camcorder to her side. Traci was laughing, too.

"We'll have to back it up and do the knife part again," Angela said. She turned to Randy and gave his ribs a hard tickle with both hands. "Thanks to you!"

"You're making a video?" Randy asked, backing away.

"We *were* until you came in," Brenda told him, climbing to her feet and pulling the bottom of her green tank top down over her jeans. "Mister Hero!" she added scornfully.

"Well, I didn't know!" Randy cried, blushing. He had Brenda's green eyes, fair skin, and freckles. But his hair was blond instead of red.

"Maybe we should leave Randy in," Traci suggested, grinning at him. She raised the camcorder to her eye and pretended to tape him. "That was a pretty real moment when he came bursting in."

"Yeah! Leave me in!" Randy urged enthusiastically. "I want to be in it!"

"No way," Brenda told him, giving him a gentle shove toward the door. "We have to follow the script."

"Why? Because *you* wrote it?" Randy shot back nastily. "If you wrote it, it stinks."

"We all wrote it," Brenda corrected him.

"Then it still stinks!" Randy declared. He pulled a can of Coke from the refrigerator. "What's it called, anyway?"

"*Night of the Jack-o'-Lantern,*" Traci told him. She set down the camcorder and smoothed back her long, black hair.

"That's dumb," Randy said, popping open the Coke can. "I should be in it."

"Just go away and let us work," Brenda told him impatiently, making shooing motions with both hands.

"I'm telling Mom you were scuffing up the floor," Randy threatened. Brenda reached out both hands menacingly and started to chase him. Randy darted out the door.

Brenda rolled her eyes. "If you look up the word *pest* in the dictionary," she told her friends, "you'll see a picture of Randy there."

Traci laughed.

"I think he's cute," Angela protested.

Brenda sighed. "That wrestling match made

me thirsty. Anybody else want a Coke?" She crossed the room to the refrigerator and began pulling out cans.

"Do you have diet?" Angela asked. She was definitely on the chubby side and always had to worry about her weight.

As she closed the refrigerator door, Brenda glanced at the kitchen knife they had used in their fake struggle — and her entire body shuddered.

"Brenda — what's wrong?" Traci asked, her dark eyes narrowing in concern.

"Ooh, I just had the *worst* flashback," Brenda told them, still shaken. She turned and led the way toward the living room. "That knife — it made me think of last year. Last Halloween. You know. Halley. And Dina. Dina stabbing me. I guess . . ." Her voice trailed off.

They sprawled comfortably in the living room. Brenda sat sideways in the big white leather armchair. Angela lowered herself onto the couch across from it and raised her feet onto the low glass coffee table. Traci sat cross-legged on the floor, resting her back against the couch.

"You shouldn't think about last Halloween," Traci said, twirling the Coke can between her hands.

"I don't," Brenda replied. "I mean, I haven't thought about Dina in weeks." She twisted her mouth fretfully. "When I do think about her . . . I . . . well, I still can't believe it. She was my best friend — and she *stabbed* me! Dina really wanted to kill me. I . . . I . . ."

"She was messed up," Traci said, staring out the window at the gathering dark clouds.

Angela sipped her diet Coke. "What happened to Dina?" she asked. Angela had moved to Fairview at the end of the summer. Since becoming Brenda's friend, she had heard only parts of the story.

"Sent away," Traci murmured.

"Her parents sent her to some hospital," Brenda added, frowning at the soda can in her lap.

"Well, don't think about last year," Traci urged. "Everything is different now."

Brenda sighed. "Not everything. Good old cousin Halley is still here."

"You and Halley aren't getting along? Again?" Traci asked, leaning back against the couch.

"Didn't you hear?" Brenda demanded. "She's going out with Ted. Isn't that sick?"

"Who's Ted?" Angela asked.

"Brenda's old boyfriend," Traci told her.

She turned back to Brenda. "But you broke up with Ted, Brenda. So what's the big deal if Halley is seeing him now?"

"I just think it's sick, that's all," Brenda replied heatedly. She turned in the chair, tossing her copper-colored braid behind her head. "Why does Halley always want whatever is mine? She took my room. She always borrows my clothes. And now why does she have to have my old boyfriend?"

"How long is your cousin living with you?" Angela asked, smoothing her hand over the couch arm.

"Forever!" Brenda wailed. "My parents got custody of Halley. She's here for good."

"Halley's parents got a divorce," Traci explained, seeing the confusion on Angela's face. "They had this horrible court fight over who got Halley. And the judge decided they were both unfit parents."

"Wow," Angela murmured. "That's really bad news."

"Tell me about it," Brenda muttered sarcastically.

"So your parents took permanent custody?" Angela asked.

Brenda nodded grimly. "Halley and I are like sisters now. At least we fight like sisters."

Angela tsk-tsked.

"We got along really well for a while," Brenda added thoughtfully. "After last Halloween. I think the whole thing with Dina and the stabbing really freaked Halley out. She was so nice to me for weeks. But after a while, she went back to her old tricks."

"She's so sexy-looking," Angela said. "I'm really jealous of all that blond hair she's always tossing around. I hate my hair." She swept one hand back through her curly brown hair.

"Your hair is okay," Traci assured her. "You should just let it grow longer. You could wear it in corkscrew curls."

"Why can't it grow straight?" Angela wailed. "Like yours," she added, reaching down and giving Traci's straight black hair a playful tug.

Traci shook her hair back into place. She glanced at her watch. "Okay. Break time is over. Ready on the set for take two!"

"Where is Jake?" Brenda demanded, glancing out the window. "Why does he always have to be late?"

"He's *your* boyfriend," Angela said with just a hint of envy in her voice. "Why ask us?"

"Do you know how many hours of my life I've spent waiting for Jake?" Brenda said, shaking her head. "He's always late. Always. And what's his excuse every time? *'I got hung up.'* Great excuse, huh?"

"Well, you know Jake," Traci murmured softly.

Brenda blinked, then stared for a moment at her friend. She had forgotten that Traci and Jake had gone together at the end of the summer. Before Brenda had started seeing him.

Of course, Jake had gone out with just about every girl at McKinley High. He never dated any girl for very long.

How long will he keep seeing me? Brenda wondered wistfully.

It had better be a long, long time.

Brenda realized that Jake had come to be very important in her life. Despite his faults, she really cared about him, cared about him more than she had ever cared about a boy.

She climbed to her feet and collected the empty soda cans. "I'll throw these in the trash. Then we can figure out where to start our fight scene again," she told her friends.

As she made her way to the kitchen, Brenda heard Traci and Angela discussing the new student teacher. "He has a great smile," Angela was saying.

"But he never smiles!" Brenda heard Traci protest.

Brenda shook her head, thinking about Jake.

She stopped at the doorway, startled to

see someone standing in the middle of the kitchen.

"Dina!" Brenda cried in shock.

And then she saw the gleaming knife in Dina's hand.

Chapter 3

Dina raised the big kitchen knife above her waist.

"Dina — please!" Brenda uttered in a hushed whisper, staring across the room in wide-eyed horror.

Dina returned her stare uncertainly. "I . . . found this on the floor," she said. "Someone must have dropped it." She set it down on the counter. "Hi, Brenda. Didn't you hear me knock?"

Brenda's heart was still racing. She made no move toward her old friend. Holding on to the door frame, her eyes studied Dina warily.

Dina was tall, at least five-ten, and very slender. Her face was pretty, but very pale, as if she had been indoors for a long time. The last time Brenda had seen her — at the Halloween party nearly a year before — Dina wore her straight brown hair cut very short.

Now, she saw that Dina had let it grow down past her shoulders.

It had a whole year to grow, Brenda thought grimly. A whole year . . .

Dina let out an awkward laugh. "Why are you staring at me like that, Brenda?" She jammed her hands into the pockets of her loose-fitting white denim jeans. She was wearing a bulky navy-blue sweater that helped emphasize how pale her skin was.

"I didn't expect . . ." Brenda started. She didn't know *what* to say. "You're back, huh?" she finally blurted out.

Dina nodded, a strange thin smile on her lips. "Yeah. I'm home. I'm starting back at school next week. I thought — "

"You — you're okay now?" Brenda asked without warmth.

"Yeah. I guess," Dina replied, lowering her eyes to the floor. "I'm seeing a shrink twice a week. I'm in the custody of my parents. I — "

She stopped as Traci and Angela appeared behind Brenda in the doorway. "Dina!" Traci cried in surprise. "Dina — you're back!"

"This is Angela," Brenda told Dina. "She just moved here."

"Hi," Angela said, not smiling.

"What is your problem?" Dina demanded,

pulling her hands from her pockets and pressing them against her waist. "All three of you are staring at me as if I'm some kind of zoo specimen!"

Brenda took a few steps into the room. "We're really surprised," she said. "We didn't expect — "

"I came right over," Dina told her. "You were my best friend, after all."

"No!" Brenda said with surprising force.

Dina's dark eyes widened. She raised one hand to her pale throat.

"No!" Brenda repeated. "No way, Dina. You're not my friend. You — you tried to *kill* me!"

She could see the hurt in Dina's eyes. She could see tears well up in the corners. She could see Dina's chin start to tremble.

But Brenda didn't care.

"Want to know something?" Dina replied softly. "I don't remember it at all. That whole night. The party. Everything. It's all erased from my mind. I don't remember a thing."

"Well, *I* do remember!" Brenda shot back heatedly. "I almost died. You wanted to kill me, Dina. You really wanted to."

A tear ran down Dina's cheek. She wiped it away with the palm of her hand. "I guess it isn't enough to say I'm sorry?"

Brenda glanced at Traci and Angela. They were huddled behind her in the doorway, their expressions tense, staring in silence at Dina.

"No, it isn't enough," Brenda said, turning back to Dina. Her mouth suddenly felt terribly dry, dry as cotton. "You can't be my friend, Dina. No way. You gave me too many nightmares, too many months of waking up terrified in the middle of the night. Too many frightening memories. You can't be my friend. You can't."

A heavy silence fell over the room.

Brenda coughed. Her throat felt so dry. She realized her hands were suddenly as cold as ice. Her legs felt weak and rubbery.

Dina opened her mouth to say something, but then quickly closed it. She turned away, as if to leave.

And then Brenda saw Dina's eyes come to rest on the kitchen knife on the counter.

No! Brenda thought, retreating, backing into Traci in the doorway.

This can't be happening! Brenda thought, watching Dina reach for the knife. *She's going to try again!*

Chapter 4

Brenda gasped as Dina's hand shot out to the knife.

Dina shoved the handle and set the knife spinning on the countertop.

Then, without glancing back at Brenda or the others, she turned and bolted out the kitchen door.

The storm door slammed shut, jolting Brenda from her frightened daze. Moving quickly to the window, she saw Dina running across the back yard, running wildly as if being chased, her brown hair flying over her shoulders.

Brenda turned back to find Traci and Angela behind her at the window.

"Weird," Angela murmured, still staring wide-eyed into the back yard even though Dina had vanished from view.

Traci shook her head disapprovingly. "You

were cold, Brenda," she said softly. "You were really cold."

Brenda scowled at Traci. "Of course I was," she replied sharply. "Why was she sneaking into my house? Why was she holding that knife? To scare me again?"

"Dina said she doesn't remember stabbing you," Traci said, picking up the camcorder and pretending to be interested in the controls. "I think she came over because . . . because she's used to hanging out here."

Brenda's cheeks flushed. "I don't care. I meant it when I said she can't be my friend." She shuddered. "She gives me the creeps just being in my house."

"I understand," Traci replied quickly.

"No, you don't. You *can't*!" Brenda accused. "You can't know what it was like — knowing that someone I trusted, someone I cared about, my best best friend, took a knife and deliberately stuck it into my chest."

Brenda's voice rose shrilly as she talked. She had to fight back the sobs that threatened to burst from her throat.

"It's okay now," Traci said soothingly, placing a hand gently on Brenda's shoulder.

"Let's talk about *this* Halloween," Angela suggested, trying to change the subject. "What should we do *this* Halloween?"

Brenda and Traci stared back at her. "I haven't thought about it," Brenda admitted.

"We should do something fun," Angela said.

Traci sighed. "We're too old for Halloween."

"No way!" Angela protested. "My parents still do Halloween. Do you believe it? They really get into it every year. They're total Halloween freaks."

"Then maybe we should go to your house," Traci suggested.

"We've never seen your house," Brenda said thoughtfully.

"You mean have a Halloween party?" Angela asked.

"No party," Brenda said sharply. She raised her eyes to the knife on the countertop. "I'm not in the mood for any Halloween party."

"Maybe just the three of us," Angela urged.

"Halloween might be canceled this year, anyway," Traci said grimly.

"Huh?" Angela reacted with surprise. "What are you talking about?"

"The town might not allow trick-or-treating this year. Because of that maniac that's prowling around," Traci said, still twirling the camcorder lens tensely. "I heard it on the news."

"They can't stop trick-or-treating!" Angela cried, shocked by the idea.

"This creep has already hurt four people," Traci told her, frowning. "Two women and two kids. He robs them. And he beats them up. He's a real sicko. Didn't you hear about him? He's a big fat guy, and he — "

"Please — stop!" Brenda raised both hands as if shielding herself from Traci's words. "First Dina, now you. You're really frightening me, Traci. Can't we talk about something that isn't scary?"

"How about Jake?" Angela suggested, grinning at Brenda.

"Jake is pretty scary," Traci commented dryly.

Brenda glanced up at the kitchen clock. "Where *is* Jake?"

Traci picked up the camcorder. "Let's try the fight scene again. I'll back up the tape to where Randy came running in. Maybe we can start where you pick up the knife, Angela, and — "

"I'm not really in the mood," Brenda interrupted. She let out a sigh. "I'm sorry. I don't feel like having a knife fight right now." She glanced out the window. "Besides, it's too dark. The sun is gone. The scene won't match up."

"I guess," Traci replied, clicking the camcorder off. "We have to go buy pumpkins, you

know. For the scary jack-o'-lantern scene at
the end."

"How about Saturday?" Brenda suggested.
"We can drive to that big farmstand on the
highway."

"Hey, are we going to the mall tonight?"
Angela asked Brenda.

"Yeah. After dinner," Brenda replied. "I'll
pick you up." She turned to Traci, who was
loading the camcorder into its black vinyl case.
"Want to come? We're just going to The Gap
and a few places. I need some sweaters."

Traci shook her head no. "Too much
homework."

A scraping sound made all three girls turn
toward the kitchen door.

Brenda gasped as the door swung open and
a figure lurched clumsily into the kitchen.

Jake! she realized. He's been beat up!

With a groan, Jake stumbled into the room.

Brenda raised both hands to her face as she
stared at him in horror.

One eye hung loose from its socket. His
cheeks were smeared with dark blood. He had
a dark, open wound in his throat with blue
veins and blood vessels dangling out like
wires.

"Help . . . please . . ." Jake choked out as
bright red blood poured from his mouth.

Chapter 5

Brenda lurched forward and caught Jake in her arms as he started to fall. Tall and broad-shouldered, he slumped against her with a groan.

As he went limp, she struggled to hold on. Traci and Angela moved quickly to help. They grabbed his shoulders and tried to pull him off Brenda.

Jake's body started to tremble all over.

Is he having convulsions? Brenda wondered.

"Jake! Jake!" Angela was screaming his name, repeating it like a shrill chant.

Jake's chest heaved as the trembling grew stronger.

And Brenda suddenly realized that Jake was laughing.

"You jerk!" she cried angrily.

Still sprawled heavily over her, he raised his

23

blood-drenched head. Then he reached up and pulled off the fake eyeball. "Gotcha," he whispered in Brenda's ear.

"Get off me!" Brenda screamed.

"Okay, okay," he said through his laughter. He leaned all of his weight on her shoulders as he pushed himself up. "Nice dancing with you."

"Oh, gross!" Traci exclaimed, backing away from Jake. "That makeup is really gross."

"Yeah." Jake grinned and opened his mouth, letting more red liquid drip to the floor.

"You scared me to death!" Angela cried, appearing pale and shaken. "I really thought —"

"I thought that maniac got you," Traci said.

"Jake is the only maniac in the room," Brenda declared bitterly. "Yuck. You got stuff all over me." She rubbed her face, then examined her red-and-blue fingers. "How are we going to clean this up? You really are a jerk."

Jake laughed. He tossed the rubber eyeball to Traci. "You should've seen the looks on your faces. Wish I'd had a camera!"

Brenda gave him a hard shove. He toppled backwards into Angela. "I thought Angela was going to *hurl*!" Jake exclaimed gleefully.

Angela started to protest. But the back door opened, and Halley stepped in. Pulling off her backpack, she smiled mischievously at them. "How's it going, guys?"

"Halley did this," Jake revealed, gesturing to the makeup on his face. "It took over an hour."

"Did they puke?" Halley asked Jake, her grin growing wider.

Jake nodded. "They thought it was real."

"Really?" Halley seemed very pleased. She pushed her disheveled blond hair back with both hands. Stepping into the room, she pulled off her blue down jacket and tossed it onto the counter.

She was wearing a tight-fitting black sweater, a short, green plaid skirt, and black tights. Brenda saw that Halley had red-and-blue makeup all over her hands.

"Jake and I got some pretty strange looks walking over here," Halley told them.

"Jake *always* gets strange looks," Traci joked.

Traci is still angry at Jake for dumping her, Brenda realized. It's so obvious.

"I thought Jake could use some scary makeup for your video," Halley told Brenda. Then she added, with some bitterness, "Just my way of contributing — since you didn't invite me to be in it."

"I — I didn't think you wanted to be in it," Brenda stammered.

She kept her eyes on Jake. Why was he spending time after school with Halley? she wondered. Whose idea was it to do the scary makeup? Was it Halley's?

She's already going out with my *last* boyfriend, Brenda thought bitterly. Is she after Jake now?

"Halley is doing the makeup for the fall play at school," Jake explained, as if reading Brenda's troubled thoughts. "I ran into her after basketball practice, and we cooked this up."

"Well, you grossed us all out," Brenda replied.

"Thanks," Halley said proudly. She lifted her bookbag off the floor. "Call me down for dinner. I've got to do some homework first. I'm meeting someone tonight." She disappeared up to her room.

Meeting someone? Brenda thought. Why didn't Halley just say she was meeting Ted?

"Oh! It's so late!" Traci exclaimed, staring up at the kitchen clock. "I've got to go."

"Me, too," Angela said. "See you after dinner, Brenda."

They hurried to the front closet to get their coats.

Jake lingered in the kitchen, admiring his reflection in the windowpane. "What are we doing for Halloween?" he asked Brenda. "Is anyone having a party or anything?"

Brenda sighed. "I really want to skip Halloween this year," she said softly. "After what happened last year . . ." Her voice trailed off.

Jake continued staring at his reflection. "Think I should get my ear pierced?" he asked.

"Huh?" Brenda, deep in thoughts about last Halloween, wasn't sure she heard correctly.

"I'd just wear like a silver band in it. Or maybe a little silver stud. It might be cool. And I'd let my hair get longer. . . ."

"Jake, you didn't hear a word I said!" Brenda cried angrily.

He finally turned away from his reflection. "What were you saying? About a Halloween party?"

She let out a groan of frustration. "I *said* I don't want to celebrate Halloween. Not after last year."

"Hey, Bren, forget last year. That's old news."

"I *can't* forget it!" Brenda confessed.

He moved quickly across the room, wrapped his strong arms around her waist, and started to lower his face to hers.

"Stop! Go away!" Brenda protested, shoving him playfully. "You'll get that gunk all over me. Stop — !"

But he was stronger than she. And she didn't really put up much of a fight.

His lips were soft and warm. He pressed them against hers tenderly at first, then harder.

As they kissed, Brenda could taste the makeup. It tasted sweet and powdery. She shut her eyes.

When he pulled his face away, Jake stared at her and laughed. "Yuck! Now we *both* look like freaks."

I don't care, Brenda thought.

I don't care about anything when you're around, Jake.

She slid her hands behind his head, and pulled him close for another makeup-smeared kiss.

"Wasn't that Gary Latchke?" Angela asked, grabbing Brenda's arm.

"I didn't see him. I was looking in that window," Brenda said, pointing.

"It's not very crowded here tonight," Angela commented. The bag slid out of her hand and clattered to the hard floor.

"Careful. You'll break your CDs," Brenda warned.

Angela bent to pick up the bag. "You can't break CDs," she replied. "They're indestructible. They'll be around as long as the planet."

They had been at the mall for twenty minutes. So far, all they had bought were some CDs that Angela had wanted.

Brenda led the way into a small boutique with a large, brightly painted carousel horse in the doorway. The store was called The Clothes Horse.

"It's all pretty tacky," Brenda complained, running her hand through a stack of gray ribbed T-shirts.

"I like the guy behind the counter," Angela confided, staring at the tall, long-haired salesclerk. "He's not too tacky."

Brenda rolled her eyes. "He's got to be in his late twenties, Angela."

Angela grinned back at her. "So?"

"You've really got boys on the brain tonight," Brenda commented, turning and making her way out of the store.

Angela said something in reply, but Brenda didn't hear her. She was hurrying across the mall to The Gap. The sweaters that interested her were in the window.

Angela went to the back to try on jeans. Brenda took her time, checking out the different sweater styles and colors, and then deciding on the first one she had seen.

She carried it to the sales counter to pay and met Angela on her way out of the dressing room. "Even the loose-fitting ones don't fit," Angela complained. "I've got to lose some weight. I've really got to."

"You should buy a pair of really tight ones," Brenda suggested, searching her bag for her wallet. "Then you should try them on each night. It would inspire you. And then think how great you'd feel when they actually fit!"

"Doing that might inspire me. Or it might totally depress me," Angela replied unhappily.

"Hey — where's my wallet?" Brenda felt a stab of dread in the pit of her stomach. She began pulling everything out of her big bag, piling it on the counter.

"Is it there?" Angela peered into the bag as Brenda pawed through everything.

"No. It's gone," Brenda told her. "Did I leave it in CD World? We've got to retrace our steps."

Brenda tossed everything back into the bag. Then she and Angela made their way out of the store, their eyes on the floor.

They crossed the mall and stopped outside

The Clothes Horse. "I didn't take my wallet out in here," Brenda recalled. "It must be at the CD store."

"It couldn't just fall out of the bag," Angela said encouragingly. "So you probably left it at the cash register."

They returned to the music store. But the cashier at CD World hadn't found a wallet.

Brenda's eyes searched the countertops, anyway. And then she tried to retrace her path between the aisles of the store.

No wallet.

Oh, wow. I'm in major trouble, she thought. I had forty dollars in my wallet and my mother's MasterCard.

A week before, Brenda had put a dent in the fender of her little blue Geo. She remembered the lecture she had received from her parents about being more responsible. And now she had to go home and tell them she lost her wallet.

Halley will *love* this, Brenda thought bitterly. She could already picture the smug, superior expression on Halley's face.

Perfect Halley. Who never lost anything.

Feeling upset and sorry for herself, Brenda lugged her bag in front of her and stepped out of the CD store. She took a few steps before noticing the man staring at her.

He was a big, fat man, Brenda saw. About thirty or forty. He stood outside the candy store across from CD World with his hands shoved deep in the pockets of his long, shabby overcoat.

His coat was unzipped, revealing an Hawaiian-style sports shirt stretched tightly over his bulging stomach, popping open so that part of his pale stomach showed through.

He had steely blue eyes set in a red balloon of a face. His white-blond hair was shaved at the sides and short on top. He had a dark scar down the left cheek. His mouth was set in a hard scowl.

Why is he staring at me like that? Brenda wondered, feeling a tremor of fear.

She glanced away, then looked back.

He was still staring with those cold blue eyes, the angry scowl frozen on his face.

Brenda turned back into the store. Angela was near the doorway, going through a stack of used CDs. "Angela — come on!" she called.

Angela didn't seem to hear her.

Brenda turned to see the fat man lumbering toward her.

"Angela — !" she shouted. She ducked into the store, grabbed Angela's arm, and tugged her away. "Run!"

"Huh?" Angela pulled back, confused.

"Run! He's coming!" Brenda cried.

Angela let out a gasp as she finally saw the frightening-looking man bouncing toward them. Without saying another word, the two girls turned and ran.

Brenda stopped short, nearly stumbling over a double baby stroller.

"Look out!" the mother cried.

The two babies in the stroller were sound asleep with their heads resting against each other.

"Sorry!" Brenda called out to their mother, and darted away.

"Hey — don't run!" she heard a man shout.

Her heart pounding, she ignored him and dodged past a group of teenagers outside the video arcade. Angela was jogging several steps ahead, nearly to the food court.

"Hey — wait up!" Brenda called breathlessly.

She turned back. Was the fat man still following?

She didn't see him.

Why was he chasing her? Why had he picked her? Why did he look so angry? Was he crazy?

Frantic questions raced through Brenda's mind as she turned a corner — and bumped into Angela.

"Whoa — sorry!" Brenda said.

But Angela, her mouth open in shock, kept staring straight ahead toward the yellow plastic tables and chairs of the food court.

"Angela — what's wrong?" Brenda demanded.

"Look," Angela murmured, pointing to a table in the corner.

Chapter 6

Brenda shuddered and drew back against the wall.

Was it the fat man? Had he somehow caught up to them?

She followed Angela's startled gaze to the food court.

And saw the couple holding hands over the yellow table.

Halley and Jake.

"No!" The word escaped Brenda's lips in a whisper.

She pressed her back against the tile wall and watched as Jake leaned over the table, pulled Halley's face to his, and kissed her.

"No. I'm not seeing this. I'm dreaming it, right?" Brenda murmured.

She felt Angela's hand grab hers. "Let's get out of here," Angela urged softly. She tugged Brenda's hand.

Brenda pulled away. "No way!" she cried angrily. "I'm going over there. I'm going to tell them both what I think of them. That they're both filthy sneaks! I'm going over there, and — "

"No," Angela insisted, pulling Brenda back around the corner. "Wait."

"Wait for what?" Brenda demanded furiously.

"Wait till you're calmer," Angela replied. "Then you can really say what you want to."

"I'll never be calmer!" Brenda wailed. "Never! How could he do this to me? This afternoon, he — he — "

"Your cousin Halley is a sicko," Angela said, frowning. "For some reason, she needs everything that's yours."

"She just hates me!" Brenda screamed, feeling herself slip out of control. "She just wants to hurt me — that's all!"

She glanced up to see an elderly couple staring at her from across the aisle. With a cry of fury, Brenda turned back to Angela. "I could tear them both apart!" she wailed. "I — I'm so hurt! I feel so totally betrayed!"

"Come on, Bren," Angela insisted, pulling Brenda back. "Let's get to the car. People are staring — "

"I don't *care*! I don't *care*!" Brenda cried.

Large tears rolled down her flushed cheeks.

Angela tugged her away. "Let's go home and talk about it. You don't want to confront them now. Why should you let Jake see how upset you are? He's a total creep. He isn't worth it."

Brenda didn't reply. But she allowed her friend to guide her toward the underground parking lot.

Tears ran down Brenda's face, but she still didn't say a word. As they walked, her features knotted tighter and tighter in anger.

I feel so betrayed, I could kill them both right now, she realized.

The upsetting thought startled her back to her senses. The store windows came back into focus. Brenda recognized a group of kids from McKinley High in front of a jewelry store. As she passed, she turned her head so they wouldn't see her tear-stained face.

I'm going to be so humiliated when everyone at school hears about Jake and me, Brenda thought with a sigh. It'll be so *horrible* when everyone hears how my own cousin stole my boyfriend. How can I ever face anyone?

"You've gotten awfully quiet," Angela said, studying Brenda's face.

"Just thinking," Brenda muttered. She followed her friend onto the elevator that led down to the parking lot. The doors slammed shut behind her, making her jump.

"Want me to drive?" Angela asked, her brown eyes wide with concern.

Brenda shook her head. "I can drive," she replied softly.

They stepped out into the concrete-walled parking lot. The walls on this level were painted sky-blue. The lot was nearly empty except for a few cars cruising slowly toward the exit.

"We're in B-4," Angela said, pointing to the signs on the posts.

Their sneakers thudded loudly on the hard surface as they made their way through the lot. Hearing the elevator doors open behind them, Brenda glanced back.

"Ohh!" She let out a startled cry as the fat man stepped out of the elevator. His eyes searched the entire area — and landed on Brenda and Angela.

"He — he found us!" Brenda stammered.

"Huh?" Angela spun around and saw the big man trotting toward them, his raincoat flapping behind him, his heavy footsteps echoing off the concrete walls.

"Run!" Brenda choked out.

But Angela was already running, several car-lengths ahead of her.

Her heart pounding, Brenda glanced back. The man's face was bright red, his eyes bulging in anger. He furiously waved both arms at them. "Hey — ! Hey — !" he shouted in a hoarse, raspy voice. His calls bounced off the walls, seemed to blare at Brenda from all sides.

Her blue Geo came into view.

She fumbled frantically in her bag and finally managed to pull the keys out in a trembling hand.

"Hurry!" Angela was screaming, her voice shrill with panic. "Hurry, Brenda!"

"Hey — ! Hey — !" The man's angry shouts echoed in Brenda's ears.

She pulled open the car door. Tossed her bag in. Dropped into the seat behind the wheel.

"Hey — ! Hey, you — !"

She heard Angela's car door slam. Out of the corner of her eye, she saw Angela gasping for breath, her chest heaving under her sweatshirt. "Hurry, Bren. Please — he's going to catch us."

Brenda fumbled with the key trying to stick it into the ignition. Her hand shook so hard, it took three tries.

Finally, the key slid in.

Brenda turned it hard.

The engine rumbled. Coughed. Then conked out.

"Hurry! Hurry!" Angela urged.

"It — it won't start," Brenda told her.

Chapter 7

She turned the key again.

The car sputtered. The engine let out a choked sound that sounded like a cough.

And then it kicked in.

"Yes!" Brenda cried gratefully, and shifted into Reverse.

"He's right behind us!" Angela warned. "He's *here!*"

"Oh!" They both cried out as the man pounded his fist on the trunk of their car.

The car bounced under the weight of his blow.

With a terrified cry, Brenda shifted into Drive. The car jolted forward with a squeal of its tires.

She floored the gas pedal and dropped back against the seat as the car shot forward.

She heard the squeal of brakes as she cut

off a car moving into the exit lane. A horn honked angrily.

But Brenda didn't slow down.

Her head hit the ceiling as she roared over a speed bump. And then another.

A sharp right turn, and they were out on the street, into the dark night, away, away, safely away. The streetlights were a soft blur in Brenda's tear-filled eyes, the center line twisting like an endless snake as she sped away from the mall.

She didn't slow the car until they approached Angela's block. As she lightened her foot on the gas pedal, she realized she'd been holding her breath the entire way. Now she let it out in a long, relieved *whoosh*.

"We should go back and report that man," Angela said, her arms crossed protectively over her chest. "He could be the maniac that we heard about on the radio."

"Why did he pick me?" Brenda demanded, thinking out loud. "Why did he chase me? Why did he seem so angry at *me*? I've never seen him before. Really!"

"He's crazy," Angela murmured, streetlights playing over her curly hair, her dark, frightened eyes catching the light. "He's crazy and dangerous. We really should report him, Bren."

Brenda's entire body shuddered. "At least we got away," she murmured, her eyes staring straight ahead through the windshield. "When he pounded on the trunk, I — I nearly jumped out of my skin."

"What a night," Angela muttered, shaking her head.

Angela's house was a ramshackle stone structure, set far back on a tree-filled front yard, surrounded by dark woods on both sides. Brenda had never been inside it. But the outside reminded her of a haunted house in a horror movie.

Angela had explained that her parents were fix-it freaks and loved to work on old houses and make them beautiful. But as Brenda slowly pulled the car up the long, sloping gravel driveway, the old house with its twin stone turrets looked cold and strangely frightening.

She stopped the car at the front walk. A porchlight over the front door cast eerie yellow light down over an enormous pumpkin resting beside the front window.

"Wow. That's a major-league pumpkin," Brenda commented, shaking her head.

"I told you — my parents are really into Halloween," Angela replied.

Angela placed a hand on Brenda's arm.

"How are you doing? Want to talk?"

Brenda hesitated. Once again she saw Jake and Halley holding hands across the yellow table.

Jake and Halley. Halley and Jake.

"Think I'll just go home," Brenda said. "Thanks, Angela."

"You sure you're going to be okay?" Angela asked with genuine concern.

"I'm a little calmer," Brenda replied. "I'm still furious and hurt and . . . and whatever." Her voice cracked. "But I don't think I want to talk about it now."

"Okay. Sorry," Angela said, pushing open the passenger door. "You didn't even get to buy your sweater."

Angela's words made the whole wretched night flash through Brenda's mind. Her lost wallet . . . the frightening, angry man . . . Jake and Halley . . .

"Things have *got* to get better!" she told Angela, forcing a smile.

I *can't* be a victim forever, she told herself darkly, feeling the anger start to build again until her entire chest burned with it.

I won't let myself be a victim forever.

Halley didn't return home for another hour and a half.

Brenda was waiting for her on the front stairs.

The lights were all out except for a dimmed spotlight in the ceiling near the coat closet. Halley didn't see Brenda at first.

Halley stepped under the light as she opened the closet door and draped her coat over a hook. Her blond hair, flung back loosely over the shoulders of her turquoise sweater, caught the light.

She keeps licking her lips, Brenda noticed, peering down at her cousin from near the top of the stairs. Chapped lips — from kissing Jake all night?

The anger surged through Brenda's body like a jolt of electrical current. She stood up.

Startled by the sudden movement, Halley raised her eyes to the stairway. "Brenda?"

"Hi, Halley," Brenda called down coldly.

"Why are you sitting there?" Halley asked, sweeping her hair back with both hands. Her blue eyes revealed her confusion.

"Waiting for you," Brenda replied, forcing her voice to stay low and steady.

"Huh?" Halley let out an awkward laugh. "I . . . was studying with someone. How long have you been sitting there?"

"A while," Brenda replied softly, her features set in a hard, cold stare.

"Well, that can't be too comfortable," Halley said.

"Not too," Brenda murmured.

Halley's expression remained calm. But Brenda could see that she was thinking hard, trying to figure out why Brenda was acting so strangely.

"Did you want to ask me something?" Halley asked, tugging tensely at a thick strand of hair.

"Yeah." Brenda nodded. "Come upstairs."

Halley hesitated.

"Come up," Brenda insisted.

"I want to get something to drink," Halley told her, licking her lips. "Some cold water."

"Come up first — okay?" Brenda coaxed, softening her tone.

Halley lowered her hand onto the wooden banister and slowly made her way up the stairs, her eyes narrowed, studying Brenda. "Why are you acting so weird, Brenda?" she demanded.

Brenda didn't reply.

When Halley was a few steps below her, Brenda moved quickly.

She leaped down, grabbed Halley's right arm, and twisted it hard behind her.

Halley didn't resist at first. "Hey — !" she cried out, laughing.

She thinks it's some kind of a joke, Brenda realized.

Well, she'll change her mind in a few seconds.

She pulled Halley's arm up hard.

"Ow — stop! You're hurting me!" Halley protested. "Let go! What is your *problem*, Brenda? What — ?"

Holding tightly to Halley's wrist, Brenda reached out with her free hand and pulled up the thick rope noose.

"Hey — !" Halley shouted as she twisted around and spotted it. "What on *earth*?!"

Brenda slipped her arm down around Halley's waist. As she held her tightly, she smelled Halley's perfume. Sweet and spicy.

Did Jake like that fragrance, Halley? Brenda wondered bitterly.

Did you wear that perfume especially for Jake? For my boyfriend?

"Let go — right now! I mean it, Brenda! This isn't funny!" Halley cried.

"No. It isn't funny," Brenda echoed. Unable to keep her feelings inside any longer, her voice broke with emotion. "It isn't funny, Halley. You're right. It's *sad*."

"Let go!" Halley squirmed and tried to pull out of Brenda's strong grasp. And as she pulled forward, her feet slipped off the stair.

"Oh!" She cried out and grabbed for the banister with both hands.

And as Halley struggled to regain her balance, Brenda slipped the noose over Halley's hair, down, down, around her neck.

"No!" Halley shrieked. "Brenda — are you crazy? Are you *crazy*?"

"It's all your fault," Brenda snapped, spitting the words, her face pressed against Halley's shoulder. "Your fault, Halley. Your fault."

"But you can't — " Halley started.

Brenda tugged on the thick rope.

Turning, glancing down, Halley's eyes bulged wide when she saw the other end of the rope tied tightly around the banister.

"All your fault," Brenda repeated, feeling the anger, the hot, hot anger surge through her, surge through every muscle. "All your fault."

"Get this off!" Halley shrieked. Gripping the banister, she ducked her head, trying to dodge away.

But Brenda held on. And as Halley struggled, the noose tightened around her throat.

"Your fault, Halley. Your fault."

Brenda tightened her arm around Halley's waist. She could feel Halley's body tremble, could feel the rapid pulsing of her heart.

Halley's hands thrashed out helplessly.

Brenda could see the red line on Halley's pale throat, the burn mark of the tightening rope.

"You're crazy! Let me go!" Halley's cry was high and shrill. And then she frantically began to call to Brenda's parents. "Uncle Michael! Help me! Aunt Eileen — please!"

"Too late, Halley," Brenda told her, feeling wave after wave of anger sweep over her. "Too late."

Chapter 8

Halley's eyes went wide with panic as Brenda tugged at the noose. Her entire body shuddered in fear, and both hands shot up to her neck as she struggled to loosen the rope.

Then, with a low groan, Brenda released her cousin. She leaned over the banister. "Did you get that, Traci?" Brenda called.

Halley was still sobbing, frantically tugging at the rope.

Holding the camcorder high, Traci stepped out from her hiding place behind the couch in the living room. "I got it all. It was great!" she exclaimed, patting the top of the camcorder.

"Good job, Halley," Brenda said cruelly. "Here. Let me help you."

She grabbed the rope with both hands and slid the noose up over Halley's head. "I didn't hurt you — did I?" she asked with false concern.

Halley's mouth dropped open as she slowly caught on. She shoved her hair back with both hands, and her expression turned from disbelief to anger.

"You — you — " Her face began to regain its color as she stammered. "This was a . . . joke?"

"Of course," Brenda replied, unable to keep a triumphant grin from spreading across her face. She realized she was dripping with sweat, and her legs felt trembly and weak.

But it was worth it, Brenda thought, her eyes locked on her cousin. It was worth it to see Halley really frightened.

"Of course it was a joke, Halley," Brenda said lightly. "You didn't really think I'd try to *hang* you — did you?"

"Shall I rewind?".Traci asked at the bottom of the stairs. "Want to see it?"

"No!" Halley screamed. "I can't believe you, Brenda. I can't believe you would do such a mean — "

"We needed a really scary scene for our video," Brenda interrupted casually. "Something real. The look on your face was *awesome*! It was so perfect!" And then Brenda added, "Actually, I thought you were just playing along, Halley."

What a lie!

Halley rubbed her throat. Brenda saw a red line burned into the pale skin. "But my neck — " Halley started.

"Did I hurt you?" Brenda asked innocently. "I'm sorry. I tried to keep it loose. I only wanted to get a good reaction — you know, for the video."

"But — but — " Halley sputtered.

"I've got to run," Traci said, winking at Brenda. "It's so late. I told my mother I was just dropping off some homework for you." She gestured with the camcorder. "Should I make a bunch of copies?"

"Don't you dare!" Halley screeched, grabbing the banister with both hands and glaring down at Traci. "You can't show that to people. You *can't*!"

"Thanks for coming by," Brenda said, ignoring Halley's protests. "See you tomorrow, Traci."

As soon as the front door closed behind Traci, Brenda turned and started up to her room. But Halley furiously grabbed her arm.

"How could you do that to me?" Halley snarled. "Have you totally lost it?"

Brenda glared back at her cousin. "Want to know the truth, Halley? Do you?"

Halley's blue eyes narrowed in anger as she tightened her grip on Brenda's arm.

"I wanted that scene to be real," Brenda confessed through clenched teeth. Her heart pounded so hard, it was difficult to talk. "I wanted the noose to be real. I wanted your fear to be real. I wanted to tighten it, and tighten it, and . . ." Her voice cracked. She let out a furious sob.

Halley let go of Brenda's arm. "What is your problem?"

"I saw you tonight," Brenda choked out, her voice just above a whisper. "At the mall. I saw you and Jake."

The light appeared to dim in Halley's eyes. She slumped down onto the step. "Sorry, Bren. It wasn't anyone's fault. It just happened."

"For sure," Brenda replied bitterly. "Like with Ted. That just happened, too — right, Halley?"

"Whoa. Hold on — !" Halley raised both hands as if to halt Brenda.

But Brenda was determined to say everything that was on her mind. She'd been holding herself in ever since Halley had moved into her house, taken over her room, become a part of the family.

But now it was too late. Too late and too much. Brenda couldn't hold back any longer.

"You want everything that's mine," she

said, forcing her voice to stay low and steady. "Everything. Look at the sweater you're wearing. It's mine. You wore *my* sweater to make out with *my* boyfriend!"

"Brenda — wait," Halley pleaded.

"First Ted. Now Jake. I really cared about Jake, Halley. I really did," Brenda cried. "But you have to take *everything* that's mine — don't you!"

To Brenda's surprise, Halley burst into tears. Sitting on the step, she lowered her head into her hands and started to cry. Her hair fell over her face. Her shoulders heaved up and down.

After a few seconds, she stopped. She turned and gazed up at Brenda through wet strands of blond hair. "Maybe I do," she said in a trembling voice. "Maybe I do want what you have, Brenda. I mean, you have everything. And I . . . I don't even have a family!"

Brenda felt a stab of regret.

Have I been too hard on her? Have I been unfair?

She had a strong urge to throw her arms around Halley's shoulders, to try to comfort her. But then Brenda pictured Halley and Jake at the mall, kissing over the yellow table.

Halley and Jake. Jake and Halley.

No, Brenda decided, overcome with bitterness. No way I'm going to try to understand poor Halley's feelings this time.

"Good night," Brenda said coldly. She started up to her room.

"You'll be sorry." Halley's words stopped Brenda short as she reached the second-floor landing.

"What did you say?" she called down.

"I said, you'll be sorry," Halley repeated in a low voice without any emotion at all.

Me? Me sorry? Brenda thought, staring down at her cousin with renewed fury. *Me?*

She's the one who should feel sorry! Brenda told herself.

How *dare* she threaten me!

She stormed down the hall to her room and slammed the door behind her. Halley doesn't know me very well, Brenda thought, standing in the middle of her room, clenching and unclenching her fists.

She thinks I'm a quiet little mouse who will put up with anything. She thinks she can steal my boyfriend and then threaten me.

She really doesn't know me very well at all.

"You'll be sorry." Halley's threat repeated in Brenda's ears.

"You'll be sorry."

Words, just words.

A few days later, the real terror began.

Chapter 9

Brenda ran into Jake the next afternoon at school. She turned the corner, heading toward chem lab, and found herself face-to-face with him.

He had a black-and-silver Raiders cap pulled over his sandy-colored hair. He wore a long-sleeved, black T-shirt pulled down over loose-fitting faded jeans, torn at one knee.

"Hey, what's up?" he asked her casually.

Brenda glared at him, shifting her backpack onto her other shoulder. Why is he grinning like that? she wondered bitterly. Can't he even *pretend* to be sorry?

She didn't say a word. She stepped past him and started toward the chem lab.

"So you . . . uh . . . heard about Halley and me," Jake said matter-of-factly, falling in step with her. Then he added lightly, "Sorry about that."

Brenda kept walking. The walls of the hallway had been decorated for Halloween. A row of big, orange, construction paper jack-o'-lanterns grinned at her as she strode past them.

Jake is grinning at me like those jack-o'-lanterns, she thought unhappily.

Is it really all a big laugh to him?

Is he such a pig that he doesn't have any idea how much he's hurt me?

"Hey, I still really like you," Jake said, waving to some friends across the hall. "Maybe we can still go out sometime."

"Maybe not," Brenda replied coldly.

Jake stepped in front of her, blocking her path. "Halley and I — we just hit it off. You know? Don't be angry, okay?"

Brenda wanted to play it cool. She wanted to seem as casual as Jake. But she couldn't. She felt too betrayed — by both of them — to stay casual.

"I *am* angry," she admitted through clenched teeth.

Her words didn't seem to mean anything to him. "Hey, bad stuff happens," he replied with a shrug. He stopped to slap a high five with a friend.

I don't *believe* him! Brenda thought miserably. I thought he *cared* about me.

"Take care," he said, giving her a little wave. He turned and hurried into the chem lab. Brenda could see Halley waiting for him inside the door.

"Oh, wow," Brenda said out loud. She pressed her back against the tile wall and shut her eyes. "Wow."

What a pig, she thought. What a total pig.

He and Halley deserve each other.

Brenda peeked into the lab. She could see Jake and Halley huddled together over a lab table.

My cousin and my boyfriend.

By now, everyone in school knows that he dumped me for her.

It's just so embarrassing, Brenda thought.

Pressing her back against the cool tile wall, she counted slowly to ten, waiting for her anger to fade, waiting for her heart to stop racing.

Then, taking a deep breath, she stepped away from the wall and turned into the lab.

Jake and Halley were so involved in each other, they didn't notice Brenda step up behind the lab table next to theirs. She dropped her backpack on the floor and climbed onto the tall lab stool.

Were all the other kids in the lab staring at her? Brenda wondered, keeping her eyes down. Or was she just getting totally paranoid?

She was grateful when Mr. Kinsolving described the day's experiment and passed out the bottles of chemicals and compounds. It meant she could concentrate on her work and not think about Halley and Jake.

She arranged the chemicals in front of her and studied the worksheet the teacher had handed out. She was checking the bottles to make sure she had everything she needed when she felt a tap on her shoulder.

"Brenda, Jake and I didn't get any sulfuric acid," Halley said. "Could we borrow a little of yours?"

"Yeah. Okay," Brenda replied curtly. The acid was in a glass test tube in her test tube holder. She lifted it carefully and held it out to Halley.

"Oh!" Halley let out a cry as the test tube slipped from her hand.

Brenda jerked her hand back — too late.

The test tube landed on the back of her hand, spilling out its liquid. Then the tube bounced onto the table, shattering loudly.

As Brenda stared down in horror, the brown liquid spread over her hand. It took a few seconds to feel the pain.

But then Brenda's hand began to burn, as if covered in hot flames. The skin peeled and curled, the burning pain grew hotter, hotter, and shot up her arm.

Then the hand started to smoke. White smoke lifting off the spreading puddle of red.

My skin, Brenda realized. It's all burning off.

And she started to scream.

Chapter 10

"You really don't think Halley did it on purpose, do you?" Angela asked.

Brenda rolled her eyes. "Of *course* she did."

Angela narrowed her brown eyes thoughtfully. She wore an oversized pale green V-neck T-shirt over a canary-yellow T-shirt and dark green denim jeans. Her dangling plastic earrings clattered with every movement of her head.

It was the afternoon after the acid "accident." They were standing in the hall, waiting for trig class to begin.

Brenda raised her bandaged hand. "I look like a mummy," she muttered, frowning.

"Does it still hurt?" Angela asked.

"It mainly itches," Brenda replied. "I thought it would hurt a lot more than it did. I mean, it looked like most of the skin was totally burned off."

"Yuck." Angela made a disgusted face.

"You're wearing lipstick," Brenda noticed, lowering the hand to her side.

Angela nodded, smiling. "My new look," she said softly.

"And new earrings," Brenda added. "I like them."

"Thanks," Angela replied, shaking her head to make them clatter. "And did you see the ring? My mom bought it for me." She stuck out her hand so that Brenda could admire the large, turquoise ring.

"Is it an opal?" Brenda asked. "It's really pretty."

Angela lowered her hand. "The new me!" she proclaimed.

"Maybe I need a new look," Brenda said, sighing wistfully. "Maybe I could keep a boyfriend if I had a new look."

"At least you *had* a boyfriend," Angela murmured. "I've never had one."

Angela's revealing statement caught Brenda by surprise. They had been friends for only a few months, since Angela had started at McKinley High.

Brenda realized that she didn't really know Angela that well. She knew that Angela hated having curly hair, that she was always trying to diet because she also hated being so chubby.

She knew that Angela had had an unhappy time at her old high school, and that she was looking forward to a fresh start here at McKinley.

Brenda knew that Angela was fun to be with, had a good sense of humor, and was a good, understanding listener.

Up to now, Brenda had confided a lot more in Angela than Angela had confided in Brenda. And so Angela's sudden admission that she'd never had a boyfriend lingered in Brenda's mind.

"I really can't believe that your own cousin would try to burn your hand off," Angela said, changing the subject.

"I do," Brenda replied quietly. "Do you believe I have to *live* with her? She practically tried to kill me, and I have to see her night and day? It — it really gives me chills. I mean, am I safe in my own house?"

Angela placed a hand on Brenda's shoulder. "Ssshhh. Don't get all worked up again. It probably was an accident, Bren. And if it wasn't, she was just paying you back for putting a noose around her neck. And now you're even."

"Even? *Even?!*" Brenda cried. She started to say more, but the bell rang.

Angela turned and made her way into the classroom. Brenda lingered behind. A stab of pain in the bandaged hand made her raise it and examine it.

When she looked up, Brenda realized that someone was watching her.

Half-hidden in shadow, Dina stood down the hall, huddled against a row of dark lockers. Still as a statue, she stared at Brenda. An icy stare. A frightening, tight-lipped expression visible on Dina's face even through the dark shadows.

"Dina?" Brenda called uncertainly in a tiny voice.

Why is she staring at me like that? Brenda wondered. Is she trying to frighten me? Is Dina still messed up?

Dina didn't reply. Didn't move.

Feeling a cold chill run down her back, feeling the coldness of Dina's stare, Brenda turned quickly away, and stepped into the classroom.

After school, Brenda hurried out without stopping to talk to anyone. Her injured hand ached. She felt tired and stressed out from thinking about Halley. Halley and Jake. Halley and Jake and Dina.

It was a warm day for October, almost balmy. In front of the school, kids had scattered their jackets and backpacks on the ground, and were talking and laughing in celebration of an extra, unexpected summery day. Several boys tossed a blue Frisbee back and forth. A little white dog yapped at their heels.

Lost in her unhappy thoughts, Brenda didn't notice the beautiful weather. She walked home quickly, staring straight ahead, and stopped on the front stoop to collect the mail.

A bright orange envelope caught her attention. It was square shaped, addressed to her: **BRENDA MORGAN**, tall letters in heavy black ink.

It looks like a card or an invitation, Brenda thought.

She shuffled through the stack of mail. Nothing else for her. Then, with only one usable hand, she had to set the mail down on the stoop to search her bag for her house key.

A few moments later, she stepped into the house, tossed her backpack onto the entryway floor, struggled out of her jacket — not easy with one hand — and carried the mail to the kitchen table.

The house was empty and silent. The only sound was the hum of the refrigerator. Bright sunlight poured through the kitchen window.

Gripping the orange envelope in her bandaged hand, Brenda used her good hand to pry it open. Was there a card inside?

No.

A square of white paper with artwork on it.

Holding it tightly in her good hand, Brenda studied it.

The drawing was crude, done in colored markers.

A big orange jack-o'-lantern filled the page. But instead of the open, jagged grin that most jack-o'-lanterns have, this one was frowning. An angry frown.

Lowering her gaze, Brenda saw that the frowning jack-o'-lantern rested in a puddle of bright red ink. Red drips rained down to the bottom of the page.

Blood? she wondered.

Is it resting in blood?

And then she saw the words scrawled in heavy black marker across the bottom:

HAPPY LAST HALLOWEEN.

Chapter 11

Mrs. Morgan tapped her fingers impatiently on the kitchen table. "Brenda, we've been over and over this," she said sternly. "We talked this all out at the emergency room, remember?"

"But I still can't make you believe me," Brenda replied, trying not to sound as desperate as she felt. "It wasn't an accident, Mom. Halley dropped the acid on me on purpose."

Mrs. Morgan sighed and rubbed her eyes. "Halley said you would believe that. She warned me."

"What?" Brenda demanded, resting her bandaged hand on the table. "What did Halley say to you?"

"She was very upset, Brenda," Mrs. Morgan replied. "She was worried about you."

"Yeah. Sure," Brenda snapped sarcastically.

"Halley came to me. She was practically in tears, Brenda. She swore to me that it was an accident. She wants you to trust her. She can't stand it that you resent her so much."

Brenda couldn't hold back a frustrated cry. "Resent her?! Mom — she stole my boyfriend from me!" she shrieked.

Mrs. Morgan shut her eyes. She gestured with both hands. "Please — lower the volume, Bren," she pleaded. "Screaming at me won't impress me."

"I'm not trying to impress you," Brenda shot back shrilly. "I'm trying to convince you that she — she's *evil*!"

Mrs. Morgan rose to her feet, scraping the kitchen chair against the floor as she stood. "It's very late," she said, glancing at the kitchen clock. "Everyone else is in bed. I think you need a good night's sleep. It will — "

"Sleep won't help me, Mom," Brenda replied heatedly. "Look. Look at this again — and tell me Halley wants me to trust her." She shoved the frowning jack-o'-lantern page across the table.

Mrs. Morgan sighed. "How many times are you going to show me that ugly thing?" she demanded. "You have no reason to accuse Halley of drawing that. It doesn't even look like something Halley would draw. It's one of your friends playing a dumb joke. That's all, Bren."

"It's not a joke!" Brenda insisted. "Saying 'Happy Last Halloween' isn't a joke, Mom. It's a threat."

"Well, why would Halley threaten you? Why?" Mrs. Morgan asked, raising her voice for the first time. "Why can't the two of you act like sisters? Why are you constantly trying to cause so much trouble over Halley?"

"Me? Me? Why am *I* causing trouble?!" Brenda shrieked, feeling herself lose control. "Haven't you listened to a word I've said?"

Without waiting for a reply, Brenda grabbed up the sheet of paper with the ugly jack-o'-lantern. Then she turned and stormed up to her room.

The next day, a gray, overcast Saturday, Brenda spent the morning closed up in her room doing homework. A little before lunchtime, a stiff breeze fluttered the curtains and rain began to patter against the windowsill.

Brenda stared blankly at the fluttering curtains, but didn't get up to close the window. The cool air feels good, she thought.

She couldn't concentrate on her government text. Why on earth did she have to know all about the Hawley–Smoot Tariff Act Trade Bill, anyway? she wondered, staring out at the rain. It's not like it will ever come up in any conversation.

She could hear Halley and Randy playing some kind of game downstairs. Halley's laughter floated up the stairs.

Brenda scowled and slammed the textbook shut. "I've got to get out of this house," she said out loud.

She pulled on a clean sweater over her T-shirt, ran a hairbrush through her coppery hair, and made her way downstairs. "I'm going to Traci's!" she shouted over the noise of the TV and Halley and Randy's loud game.

No one seemed to care.

Brenda slipped her raincoat over her shoulders, grabbed her bag, and hurried out the door.

Traci's house was a five-minute drive. But Brenda cruised around town for a while, driving aimlessly. She listened to the click and scrape of the windshield wipers, staring out into the gray afternoon, trying not to think about Halley and Jake, trying to make her mind a blank.

Nearly an hour later, she pulled up the smooth asphalt driveway and peered out at

Traci's house. It was a long, low, redwood ranch-style house. A row of small evergreen trees lined the walk that led to the front door.

Brenda pushed open the car door and climbed out. The rain had slowed to a drizzle. The dark driveway was dotted with shimmering rainwater puddles. The cold wind felt sharp against her cheeks as she made her way to the bright red front door.

Brenda rang the bell. Traci's mother appeared a few seconds later. She had Traci's straight, black hair and dark eyes. "Hi, Bren," she said, motioning for Brenda to come in. "Traci didn't say you were coming."

"I was driving around," Brenda explained. "Is she home?" She peered into the house. The aroma of a roasting chicken floated from the kitchen.

"She'll be back in a few minutes," Mrs. Warner said, helping Brenda tug off her jacket. "She just went to the store for me. I'm feeling ambitious today. I'm actually cooking dinner."

"Smells great," Brenda commented, taking a deep sniff.

"You can wait in Traci's room if you want," Mrs. Warner said.

Brenda thanked her and made her way down the familiar hall to Traci's room at the end.

Traci is so lucky, Brenda thought. No noisy little brother. No cousin living with her, making her life miserable.

She stepped into Traci's bedroom, and her eyes glanced quickly around. One entire wall was covered with posters and photos cut out from magazines, faces of rock singers and the movie stars Traci liked.

The bed was neatly made. The window behind the bed was spotted with raindrops. The closet door was open a crack, revealing shelves of neatly folded T-shirts and sweaters.

Brenda was on her way to the bed, planning to sit down and wait for her friend — when something on Traci's desk caught her eyes.

"Oh, no! I don't *believe* it!" Brenda cried out loud when she recognized what it was.

Chapter 12

Brenda stared at the sheets of paper on the desk and the orange and black markers lying beside them.

Orange and black markers with their caps off. A red marking pen standing upright behind them.

The big orange jack-o'-lantern with its ugly frown, its puddle of red blood, its scrawled threat, reappeared in Brenda's mind.

She flipped quickly through the sheets of paper. All blank.

She reached for the orange marker when Traci burst into the room. "Hi, Bren. How *are* you?" Traci asked brightly, tossing her yellow rain slicker onto the bed. "Mom said you — "

Brenda raised the orange marking pen and waved it in Traci's face. "How *could* you?" she demanded.

73

"Huh?" Traci's mouth dropped open in shock. She shook her straight black hair behind the shoulder of her blue-and-white tank top.

"How could you send that ugly thing to me, Traci?" Brenda accused her angrily.

"My card? I just mailed it," Traci replied, narrowing her eyes suspiciously at Brenda. "You couldn't have gotten it that fast."

"You *admit* it?" Brenda cried shrilly. "You admit that you sent it to me?"

Traci continued staring at her friend. "Brenda, are you okay? I told you, I just mailed my Halloween cards out a few minutes ago. When I went to the store for my mother."

"Cards?" Now it was Brenda's turn to feel confused.

"It was such a dreary, rainy day. I thought it would be fun to draw some silly cards and send them out," Traci explained. "I really don't understand why you — "

"Oh, wow," Brenda muttered. "I thought — well, I saw the markers and . . ." Her voice trailed off.

How could I suspect Traci? Brenda asked herself, feeling embarrassed and upset.

What is *wrong* with me?

She quickly explained about the ugly drawing she had received in the mail.

"That sounds like something your *brother* would do!" Traci exclaimed.

Brenda shook her head. "No. It had to be Halley. It had to be. Halley is definitely on the warpath," Brenda said sadly.

"She took your boyfriend away. Then she practically burned your hand off. Wasn't that enough?" Traci asked, rolling her eyes.

Before Brenda could reply, the phone on the desk rang.

Traci picked it up after the second ring. She talked for a few seconds, then turned to Brenda. "It's Angela. Want to go over to her house and work on our video project?"

Brenda nodded. "Sure. Why not? It's a dark, gloomy day. Perfect for making a horror movie."

In the gray light, Angela's ramshackle house with its twin stone turrets looked more like a haunted house to Brenda than ever. As she and Traci climbed out of the car, the old trees rattled in the gusting wind like skeleton bones.

Rainwater poured from a broken gutter above the front stoop. It splashed noisily onto the broken flagstone walk.

"Angela's parents are fixer-uppers," Brenda explained, seeing the surprised expression on Traci's face.

"When are they going to start?" Traci joked.

Stepping around the gutter waterfall, they made their way to the front stoop. The house was dark. The big, round pumpkin in the corner by the door had large drops of rainwater running down its sides.

Brenda rang the doorbell. She pushed it three times. "Doesn't seem to be working. I don't hear anything," she told Traci.

Traci pulled open the storm door. Brenda knocked loudly with her fist.

To her surprise, the force of her knock pushed the door partway open.

"Angela?" Brenda called, leaning in. The front entryway was dark. "Angela? Where are you?"

No reply.

A sharp wind gust pushed the heavy door open a little more. It creaked as it swung in.

"Creepy," Traci muttered, gripping the camcorder case tightly in one hand. "We should try to use that sound in our video."

"Angela?" Brenda called, cupping her hands like a megaphone.

The door creaked open a bit further, revealing more of the dark, bare entryway.

Brenda stepped inside. Traci followed.

"Anybody home?" Traci's voice sounded hollow in the bare hallway.

Brenda waited for her eyes to adjust to the darkness. Then she started toward the front room. "Angela must be in back," she said. She shouted again: "Angela? Where are you?"

"Wow. Doesn't anyone ever dust in here?" Traci whispered.

Brenda followed Traci's gaze to the cobwebs, as thick as a curtain, at the top of the living room doorway. An enormous black spider, its wiry legs straddling a dead fly, rested like a bull's-eye in the center of one web.

"Yuck," Brenda murmured. Glancing down, she saw that her sneakers were scraping through a thick layer of dust on the dark floorboards. "I can't believe that Angela's parents don't ever dust or vacuum. I mean — "

Brenda stopped short as she spotted the coffins.

Two of them. Side by side in the center of the living room.

"Oh, no!" Traci grabbed Brenda's arm. "What on earth — !"

"Angela!" Brenda shouted. "Angela — where *are* you?"

No reply.

The wind made the panes rattle in the large front window. In the gloomy gray light from the dust-smeared window, Brenda saw that the living room was nearly as bare as the entryway.

The two black coffins stood in the middle of the room. Two straight-backed wooden chairs were on either side of the window. The mantelpiece over the fireplace held a tall wooden clock, its hands stuck at twelve-fifteen.

Beside the clock, in the very center of the mantel, a single candle burned. Wax rolled down its sides. Its pale light flickered and dipped from the breezes through the rattling window.

"I — I don't like this," Traci murmured, holding on to Brenda's arm. "These coffins — "

"I don't get it. How can Angela live like this?" Brenda said, her eyes searching the dark, dust-covered room.

"Angela! Angela!" Traci screamed. She turned to Brenda. "Think we should look upstairs?"

Brenda started to reply — but stopped when she saw the hand.

"Ohhh." She let out a low gasp of horror.

"What? What is it?" Traci demanded. Then she saw it, too.

The coffin lid on the left was open a crack. And a hand dangled limply from inside the coffin.

Squinting in the gray light, Brenda hesitated, then took a reluctant step toward the coffin.

As she moved closer, the dangling hand came into focus, and Brenda saw the polished orange fingernails and the ring on the third finger. The opal ring.

"Oh, no, Traci!" Brenda moaned. "It's Angela in there."

Chapter 13

Traci's eyes bulged, and a strange, rattling sound escaped her throat.

Brenda swallowed hard, struggling against the waves of nausea that swept up from her stomach.

A creaking sound, followed by the loud *slam* of the front door, made both girls cry out.

Brenda stared hard at Angela's pudgy, pale hand. The new opal ring caught the gray light from the window and gleamed darkly.

"The police — " Traci choked out. Her entire body shuddered. The camcorder case fell from her hand and hit the floor with a *thud*.

"Yes," Brenda agreed. "There's got to be a phone."

"Maybe . . . we should get out of here," Traci urged. "Maybe whoever did this . . . is still here." She shuddered again.

They both froze. And listened.

The windowpanes rattled. No other sound.

Brenda turned back to the lifeless, pale hand. The entire room around it suddenly blurred. The coffins, the dust, the cobwebs, the bare walls — all cloudy like a heavy gray mist.

She blinked. Once. Twice.

The room slowly sharpened back into focus. And Brenda realized she was staring across the room into a den. And seated on a low couch in the den, leaning against each other in an almost cozy pose, were two skeletons.

Two human skeletons.

Brenda didn't realize she was screaming until her high-pitched shriek had nearly ended. It escaped from her throat like the cry of a trapped animal.

She cut the cry short when the coffin lid began to rise.

Slowly, slowly, the heavy lid lifted.

Brenda wanted to scream again — but she was shaking too hard to make a sound.

Chapter 14

Brenda grabbed on to Traci. The room blurred again as the coffin lid slowly opened.

And Angela, grinning, lifted herself out.

"Happy Halloween!" she cried, straightening the white sweatshirt she wore, pulling it down over her loose-fitting jeans.

As Brenda and Traci goggled in amazement, still trembling, still gasping for breath, Angela let out a gleeful, triumphant laugh.

"You — you — " Traci struggled to find words.

"You really *terrified* us!" Brenda finally managed to choke out. Then, suddenly, her anger burst from her in a torrent of words. "How could you *do* that to us, Angela? You really have a sick sense of humor! This room — these coffins — !"

"It's sick! Really sick!" Traci agreed in a trembling voice. "We thought you were — "

Angela shook her head, still grinning. Her dark eyes glowed in the dim light. Behind her on the mantelpiece, the candle flickered out. The room grew even darker.

"I *told* you my parents were really into Halloween!" Angela declared brightly, enjoying her triumph. "I really didn't mean to scare you *that* bad. I thought you would guess."

"Guess what?" Brenda demanded angrily. "Guess that you're a nutcase?"

Angela's grin faded. Brenda could see the hurt in her eyes. "It was just a joke," Angela said quietly. "I really didn't think you'd take it seriously."

Brenda scowled. Traci appeared dazed.

Angela stepped between them and put her arms around their shoulders. "I'm sorry. Really," she said. "I thought you'd guess. I told you about my parents."

Brenda let out a long sigh. Her heart had slowed to normal. She was starting to feel better.

"But the cobwebs," Traci insisted, shaking her head as if trying to clear it. "And all the dust. And no furniture."

"My parents did it all," Angela explained, her arms still around them. "They do it every year. Carry all the furniture down to the basement, and bring up the two coffins. Then they spray on the cobwebs and the dust and stuff."

"It's so . . . creepy," Brenda said softly, gazing at the open coffin. The insides were covered in a dark purple satin. She suddenly wondered what it would feel like to lie in there and pretend to be dead, as Angela had done.

"They've still got lots to do," Angela continued. "And, of course, I help them. We still have to do the lighting. Really eerie lighting. And the jack-o'-lanterns. We always have lots of great-looking jack-o'-lanterns. And we also — "

"Where did you get the skeletons?" Traci interrupted, pointing toward the den.

Angela laughed. "Those old guys? They've been in the family for as long as I can remember. Aren't they great?"

"Yeah. Great," Brenda muttered sarcastically, rolling her eyes. The two skeletons, leaning against each other, grinned back at her.

"What a shame we didn't get the whole thing on tape," Angela said, shaking her head. "It would have been *awesome*! You guys want a Coke or something?"

"Yeah. My mouth is kind of dry," Brenda replied. "From screaming."

Angela chuckled as she led them to the kitchen.

"Hey — a normal-looking room!" Brenda cried, glad to see clean wood counters and gleaming kitchen appliances.

"Mom and Dad don't decorate the kitchen," Angela said, pulling open the refrigerator and bending to drag soda cans off the bottom shelf.

"Are your parents home?" Traci asked. "I've never met them."

"Me, either," Brenda said. "I want to tell them what a great job they did in the living room. I mean, the whole thing nearly scared me to death."

"I'll tell them you liked it," Angela replied, her eyes lighting up. "They're not home."

Traci took a long drink from the soda can. "Mmmm. I feel a lot better," she said, smiling for the first time since she and Brenda had entered the house.

"Me, too," Brenda agreed. "Well . . . you put us in a good mood for horror, Angela. Let's start taping."

"Do you think Angela is weird?"

Brenda shifted the cordless phone to her other ear and leaned back against the headboard. It was Sunday night. She had finished her homework. Now she was stretched out on top of her bed, talking on the phone to Traci.

"How do you mean weird?" Traci asked.

"I mean, lying in that coffin like that," Brenda continued. "Deliberately scaring us out of our minds."

"It was just a dumb joke," Traci replied. Brenda could hear her bubble gum pop. "She said she thought we'd figure out it was a joke."

"But she could hear us," Brenda insisted. "She could hear how frightened we were. She could hear us screaming."

"Yeah. True," Traci agreed thoughtfully.

"So do you think she's weird?" Brenda repeated.

Traci laughed. "I think everyone is weird!"

"She seems really nice," Brenda continued. "I mean, smart and funny and everything. But we don't really know her that well."

"Angela is okay," Traci said, popping another bubble. "So what else is up with you, Bren?"

Brenda sighed. "What could be happening with me? Halley went out with Jake last night. I sat home and baby-sat Randy. Today I spent most of the day feeling sorry for myself and doing homework. It took me hours to read those chapters in *The Iliad*. All that fighting."

"Yeah, I know," Traci agreed. "I couldn't keep one soldier straight from another. Wish there was a movie of it I could rent."

"Halley spent the whole day avoiding me," Brenda continued. "Every time she passes me, she looks right through me, like I'm not there."

"Nice," Traci commented sarcastically.

"She went out again this afternoon," Brenda said. "Probably with Jake." She sighed.

"Cheer up," Traci urged. "Jake isn't that great. Really."

"That's what I keep telling myself," Brenda revealed. "I mean, he was so terrible to me. He acted as if I didn't mean a thing to him. Like I was a bug or something. I'm better off without him. That's what I tell myself over and over. But then I think about him with Halley, and I get upset all over again."

"He's a creep," Traci said. Brenda could hear shouting in the background. "I've got to get off. My mom wants to use the phone."

"Okay. See you tomorrow," Brenda said.

"Tomorrow," Traci repeated. "Tomorrow will be better, Bren. You'll see."

"Yeah. Better," Brenda echoed. "Much better."

But it wasn't.

The next morning, the vest she wanted to wear over her white T-shirt had a stain on the front. She had to change her whole outfit.

Then she couldn't find her hairbrush.

She hurried down to breakfast. Randy was finishing his Froot Loops. Her parents were reading sections of the newspaper, sipping from white mugs of coffee.

"Where's Halley?" Brenda asked, yawning. She popped two slices of bread into the toaster.

"Went to school early," Mr. Morgan replied from behind the paper.

"She left a long time ago," Randy reported. He had an orange juice mustache over his upper lip.

"Weird," Brenda muttered, finding the butter in the refrigerator.

"What are you doing after school?" Mrs. Morgan asked Brenda. "Can you come home and watch Randy?"

"I don't *want* her to watch me!" Randy protested, scooping up the last Froot Loop.

"Yeah. No problem," Brenda told her mother. "Traci and Angela are coming over to finish our video. We can watch Randy at the same time."

"I want to be in it!" Randy insisted. "I want to fight somebody!"

Brenda ignored him and gulped down her breakfast. Then she pulled on her jacket, hoisted her backpack over her shoulder, and hurried to McKinley High.

The halls were already emptying as Brenda made her way to her locker. The bell for home room was about to ring.

Brenda started to slide the backpack to the floor when she caught her first whiff of the odor.

A sour odor.

She sniffed again.

"Yuck." It was more than sour. It was *rotten*.

"Oooh. What is that?" Brenda asked Lauren Taylor, a girl from her class who was pulling a trapper-keeper from the locker across the hall.

"Smells like rotten meat or something," Lauren said, holding her nose.

"Oh, wow. It's really gross," Brenda said, making a disgusted face. She held her breath as she set down her backpack.

The odor was overwhelming.

"Where is it coming from?" she cried, glancing back at Lauren.

Lauren slammed her locker shut. "The lunchroom, probably," she joked. She waved and hurried to home room.

Brenda didn't think it was funny. The

smell was so powerful, so putrid.

She turned the combination lock. Pulled open her locker.

Stared inside.

Stared in horror and disbelief at the jack-o'-lantern frowning up at her. The rotted pumpkin flesh, blanketed in a heavy coating of green and blue mold, was covered with crawling maggots.

Brenda inhaled another breath of it.

And then started to retch.

Chapter 15

"The horrible stink will never leave!" Brenda wailed. "I'll be smelling it for the rest of my life!"

"Mr. Connelly scrubbed your locker for hours," Traci said. "It *can't* smell anymore!"

"But it does," Brenda insisted miserably. "Besides, the smell is in my nose. It's trapped in there. Forever." She made a sick face. "I can smell it right now."

Randy let out a gleeful laugh and slapped his sister on the back. "Wish I could have seen it!" he cried.

The three of them were sitting around the kitchen table, chewing on fat pretzels and drinking tall glasses of apple juice. Brenda and Traci were waiting for Angela to get out of chorus practice and join them for the last taping session of *Night of the Jack-o'-Lantern*.

"What did it smell like?" Randy demanded,

grinning. "Did it smell like a skunk?" He dropped off his chair and came up behind Brenda. "Did it?"

"It smelled like your closet," Brenda replied, giving him a playful shove.

"I'm going upstairs and play Nintendo," he announced.

"Do you have homework?" Brenda called after him.

"I don't know!" he shouted back. For some reason, Randy never knew if he had homework or not.

As soon as he was out of the room, Traci leaned close to Brenda and spoke in a low voice. "Did you confront Halley? Did you tell her you knew she did it?"

Brenda nodded and lowered her eyes. "We had a horrible scene in the lunchroom. It was so embarrassing. The only good thing was I embarrassed her, too."

Traci licked some of the salt off her pretzel. "And Halley denied it?"

"Of course," Brenda replied glumly. She raised her juice glass, but then didn't drink any. "It had to be Halley. Why else would she leave the house so early this morning? It *had* to be my sweet cousin." She set down the glass and gazed blankly out the window.

"Are you going to tell your parents?" Traci asked.

"What for?" Brenda moaned. "They think Halley is perfect. They don't want to hear any complaints. If I tell them that Halley shoved a rotted, maggot-infested pumpkin in my locker, my parents will just accuse me of trying to start trouble." She let out a grim, mirthless laugh.

Traci started to reply, but Angela came bursting into the room, breathing hard. "Sorry I'm so late. But Miss Andersen kept the whole chorus rehearsing. It wasn't *staccato* enough." Angela sighed. "It's *never* staccato enough."

"Want a pretzel?" Brenda raised a pretzel in Angela's general direction.

Angela shoved it away. "You know I'm trying to diet." She gestured to her plump body. "Do I look like I need a pretzel?"

"One pretzel can't hurt," Brenda replied distractedly.

"Hey — did you know Halley and Jake are out front?" Angela asked. "They're having a fight."

"Huh?" Brenda's mouth dropped open. "Are they really?"

Angela nodded, a pleased grin rapidly spreading across her round face.

Traci scooted her chair back. "Quick — I'm getting the camcorder."

"What are you going to do?" Brenda demanded, climbing to her feet.

"I'm going to tape their fight," Traci said, bending to pull the camcorder from its case. "This could be excellent!"

Brenda smiled for the first time all day.

"If Jake sees you, he won't be happy," Angela warned. "He once told me how much he hates being embarrassed."

Brenda flashed Angela a suspicious glance. "When did Jake tell you that?"

Angela's round cheeks turned pink. "A few weeks ago. Jake and I were waiting for you. At the mall. Remember?"

"Oh. Right," Brenda replied.

"Well, Jake and I started talking about the things we hated most," Angela continued. "And he said he hated being embarrassed more than anything else."

Traci snickered as she slung the camcorder strap over her shoulder. "Let's see if we can *really* embarrass him! Come on. Hurry — before they make up."

"I really think this is a bad idea," Angela warned.

But Brenda and Traci were already running to the front. Traci slipped out the front door and made her way quickly behind a tall ever-green shrub beside the stoop.

Brenda hesitated, holding on to the glass storm door. Then she followed Traci, bumping her as she squeezed between the shrub and the front of the house.

Safely hidden, Brenda turned her eyes to the driveway. Jake's red Bonneville was parked in the drive. Jake, in a gray hooded sweatshirt and black denim jeans, leaned against the hood as Halley paced in front of him in the driveway.

Halley kept tossing her blond hair back and gesturing angrily with both hands. Jake had his arms crossed in front of him and wasn't saying much.

"I can't hear," Brenda whispered. "What are they arguing about?"

"A girl named Teresa, I think," Angela whispered. She had followed them outside and was pressed behind the trunk of the old maple tree near the driveway.

"Ssshhh!" Traci raised a finger to her lips. "I'm taping." She held the camcorder to her eye as she leaned out from behind the tall evergreen.

Brenda turned back to the driveway and struggled to hear what they were saying. Jake was vigorously shaking his head no, a tight frown on his face. Halley had stopped pacing and stood in front of him, very close. She had her back to Brenda, but her gestures revealed how angry she was.

"I only had one date with her!" Jake's words floated from the driveway.

So it *is* about another girl, Brenda thought with some satisfaction. She leaned forward, trying to hear more.

But a loud cry interrupted. "Brenda! Brenda — come here!"

Randy. Shouting from inside the house.

"Brenda! Brenda — where *are* you?"

Randy is going to spoil everything, Brenda thought. She turned and crept into the house, hoping Jake or Halley wouldn't see her. Closing the storm door silently behind her, she took a few steps into the living room.

"Randy — where are you? What do you want?" she called.

"I'm in my room!" he shouted down.

Brenda hurried to the stairs. "Well, what's wrong? Why did you call me?"

Her brother appeared at the top of the stairs, a comic book in one hand. "I need something to drink."

"Huh? You called me into the house because you need a drink? Why don't you get it yourself?" Brenda cried angrily.

"I'm reading. Can you get it for me? Can you get me a box of juice?" Randy demanded.

"Aaaaagh!" Brenda let out a frustrated cry. "You are a lazy bum!" she shouted. But she turned and started to the kitchen to get him his juice.

What a spoiled brat, she thought, shaking her head.

Brenda was halfway to the kitchen when she heard shrill cries outside.

"Hey — let go! Stop it, Jake!"

It's Traci! Brenda realized, stopping and turning back toward the front door.

Traci's cries grew more angry. "Jake — let go! I mean it! Stop! Stop it!"

And then Brenda heard Traci let out a long, high-pitched scream.

Chapter 16

With a frightened cry, Brenda lunged to the front door, shoved it open, and burst outside. "What's going on?" she demanded loudly.

Jake and Traci stood facing each other in front of the car. Halley and Angela stood tensely a few feet away on opposite sides of the driveway.

"What's wrong?" Brenda demanded.

No one moved. No one seemed to hear her.

Traci, Brenda saw, had the camcorder nestled under one arm. She had one hand outstretched and was gesturing wildly to Jake. "Give it back! Give it to me!"

Jake held the tape cassette in one hand, and was unraveling the tape with his other hand, stretching it, pulling it out.

Traci made a grab for it. But Jake dodged back out of her reach. Then he dropped the plastic cassette case on the driveway — and tromped on it hard with the heel of his shoe.

"Here! You want it?" Jake's face turned an angry red. He picked up the cracked cassette and shoved it into Traci's hands.

"But this is our project!" Traci shrieked at him. "This is our project for school!"

"I don't like to be embarrassed," Jake said through clenched teeth.

"But it's our project! It's our project!" Traci repeated frantically, staring at the ruined video cassette.

Halley and Angela watched in silence.

Brenda stood on the front walk, her hands balled into tight fists. How could he do that to us? she wondered, feeling her anger tighten every muscle in her body. How?

How could he be such a creep?

She watched Jake turn and stride quickly to his car, the hood of his sweatshirt bobbing up and down as he walked. Climbing in, he slammed the door shut behind him. A few seconds later, the car shot down the driveway and screeched away.

"It's our project! He wrecked our project!" Traci cried, holding the broken cassette up to show Brenda. "What are we going to do?"

Brenda turned to her cousin. "Halley — ?"

Ignoring her, keeping her cold blue eyes straight ahead, Halley brushed past Brenda and disappeared into the house without saying a word.

Brenda, Traci, and Angela exchanged unhappy glances. Then the three of them trudged into the house.

They sprawled in the living room. Traci dropped onto the couch, the broken cassette still in her hand. She pulled at the unraveled tape until she had a big handful of it, then glumly tossed the whole thing to the floor.

Brenda and Angela slumped into armchairs across from Traci. "What are we going to do?" Brenda asked, staring down at the pile of ruined videotape.

"Start all over again, I guess," Angela replied quietly.

"No. I mean about that creep Jake," Brenda said. "What are we going to do about Jake?"

Traci's dark eyes lit up. Her expression brightened as a thin smile played over her lips. "Hey, I know," she said cheerfully. "Let's kill him!"

Chapter 17

Of course no one took Traci seriously.

But they were still talking about her idea in the lunchroom the next day.

"Just how great would it be?" Traci was saying, stirring the blueberries at the bottom of her yogurt container. "I mean, if we made Jake think we were really going to kill him — and we got it all on tape?"

Brenda laughed. "You're sick, Traci. You really are." And then she added, "I guess that's why I like you."

All three of them laughed at that.

"We get Jake on tape, looking scared out of his mind," Traci continued with enthusiasm. "Maybe he's pleading with us, *begging* us. Maybe he's crying."

"Maybe he's promising to change, to become a better person," Brenda suggested, unwrapping her tuna fish sandwich. "That would be good."

Traci swallowed a spoonful of yogurt. "We get it all on tape. We make a zillion copies. Maybe we give one to every kid in school." She grinned. "And poor Jake is embarrassed — for life!"

Brenda and Traci slapped each other a high five.

"You're awfully quiet," Brenda said to Angela.

Angela hadn't touched her salad. "Just thinking," she replied, forcing a smile. "I guess we should do this at my house."

"Yeah. Right!" Traci and Brenda immediately agreed.

"We can use the coffins!" Brenda suggested. "They're so scary to begin with."

"Maybe I could lie in one," Angela said, thinking hard. "You know, the way I did when you two came over. Maybe I could scare Jake the way I scared you."

"Excellent," Traci replied. "Excellent!"

"But it isn't enough," Brenda told them. She took another bite of her sandwich, her eyes moving around the crowded room. "Hey, look," she whispered. "Over there."

She motioned to the table in the corner where Dina sat, eating lunch by herself.

"Why is she staring at us like that?" Traci asked, turning her head to see Dina.

"She's staring at *me*," Brenda replied. "Every time I see Dina, she just gives me that hard stare, like she's trying to frighten me or something."

"She's in my government class," Traci revealed. "But we never speak to each other." She sighed. "It's like we were never friends."

"Look at her. Sitting all by herself. Just staring," Brenda whispered. She felt a chill run down her back.

It had been an entire year since Dina had stabbed her at the Halloween party. But Brenda realized she hadn't really gotten over it. She was still terrified of Dina.

She really wished Dina hadn't come back to school.

"Don't pay any attention to her," Angela was saying. "Brenda? Earth calling Brenda!"

Brenda snapped out of her unhappy memories. "Let's get back to our plan," she said, taking a sip of her Coke. "How do we terrify Jake? We have Angela in the coffin?"

"That's not enough," Traci commented, scraping up the last drops of yogurt from the bottom of the carton. "We want him to be *really* terrified. I mean, 'Call for Mommy' terrified — right?"

Brenda and Angela laughed.

"Mommy! I want my mommy!" Brenda imitated Jake crying for his mother.

"So maybe we should tie him up or something," Traci suggested, taking a handful of Brenda's potato chips from the bag. "Maybe make him think we're going to torture him."

"No. We have to make him believe we're going to *kill* him," Brenda said. "We really have to make him believe. We want the camcorder to pick up those beads of sweat on his forehead. We want to see him squirming and shaking."

"I *love* this!" Traci declared. "This is great even if we don't do it!"

Angela laughed.

Brenda remained serious. "But we're going to do it, right? We're really going to do it?"

"Right," Traci said, her smile fading.

"Right," Angela added, making it unanimous.

They made a date for after school to make further plans. There were lots of details to work out, Brenda realized. Lots of problems.

The biggest problem was how to lure Jake to Angela's house.

That's not exactly going to be easy, she realized.

Traci and Angela had gym the period after lunch. They hurried off to get changed. Brenda lingered over her lunch, thinking about how nice it would be to pay Jake back for dumping her in such a cold way and for deliberately ruining their class project.

She gathered up all the aluminum foil and plastic wrappers, and tossed it all in the trash. Then she stopped to talk with some friends.

By the time she made her way to the door, the lunchroom was nearly empty. The bell for fifth period was about to ring any second.

Brenda stepped out into the hallway. She turned toward the stairs that led up to her locker — and felt strong hands go around her waist.

"Hey — " she gasped.

The strong hands spun her around.

"Jake — what do you want?" Brenda cried.

Chapter 18

Jake grinned at her, bringing his face close, his hands holding on to her waist. "Miss me?" he asked.

"Huh? Are you crazy?" Brenda tried to struggle free. But Jake held on tightly.

His blue eyes locked on hers. His sandy hair fell over his forehead.

He's trying to look sexy, Brenda realized. I really don't *believe* this!

"What do you want, Jake?" she demanded.

"To apologize," he replied, surprising her. "I mean . . . you and I, Bren . . . we had a good thing, you know? And I . . . blew it."

"Yeah," Brenda replied. Not much of a comeback, she told herself. But he had caught her completely off-guard. She didn't know *what* to say.

Jake brought his face closer. His breath

smelled of peppermint. "I thought maybe you and I . . ." His voice trailed off.

"Listen, Jake — " Brenda started.

But before she could tell him to get lost, he moved his hands up to her shoulders, pulled her closer, and lowered his mouth onto hers.

Brenda ended the kiss quickly and tried to back out of his grasp. "Let go, Jake," she said sharply. "People are watching."

"Who cares?" he replied, grinning.

He kissed her again.

She raised both hands to his chest to push him away — but then had an idea.

If Jake thinks I'm still interested in him, Brenda thought, it'll be easier to get him to Angela's house on Halloween.

In fact, if Jake thinks we're going together again, it'll be a *breeze* to get him to Angela's.

Leaving her hands against the front of his sweater, Brenda returned the kiss.

He's so good-looking, she thought. And he's such a good kisser.

I cared about him. I really did.

But not anymore.

He hurt me too much.

The bell jangled loudly, causing them both to break away.

Jake grinned at her. "I had a feeling you

missed me!" he boasted. "I mean, so I made a little mistake. Big deal, right?"

"Yeah," Brenda agreed, forcing a smile.

"Maybe you and I could do something Saturday. You know. Halloween," he said.

"Sounds good," Brenda replied. Her smile grew wider. Then she added slyly, "Maybe we'll do something *scary!*"

"I don't believe it! This is excellent!" Traci declared when Brenda told her the news. Angela didn't say a word. She appeared to be struck speechless.

They had gone directly to Brenda's house after school to plot and try to scheme a way to get Jake to Angela's house. Now they sat around the kitchen table, sharing a gooey frozen pizza Brenda had heated in the microwave, amazed that Jake had played right into their hands.

"Jake even suggested doing something on Halloween," Brenda reported, pulling a string of white cheese off her chin. "Do you believe it?"

She and Traci slapped each other a high five. Angela continued to stare in amazement.

Suddenly, Traci's expression turned suspicious. She dropped her pizza slice onto the plate and narrowed her eyes at Brenda. "Hey, you're not really going back with Jake — are you?"

Brenda swallowed. "Of course not, Traci. Do you think I'm crazy?"

"Just asking," Traci replied quickly. She picked up her slice.

"So what do I tell him?" Brenda asked them, her green eyes lighting up mischievously. "Do I tell him you're having a party, Angela? And that he and I are invited?"

"That might work," Angela replied thoughtfully.

"A costume party," Traci suggested. "It'll be funny to get Jake in some dumb costume, and then torture him and scare him out of his mind."

"What if we all go trick-or-treating?" Brenda suggested.

"Huh? We're too old!" Angela protested.

"No way! We're not too old. It might be fun," Traci commented.

"What if I tell Jake that the three of us are going trick-or-treating, and I invite him to join us?" Brenda said. "Then we just sort of happen to end up at Angela's house."

"Sounds good," Traci told her, taking the last bite of her pizza slice, wiping her hands on a paper napkin.

"Then Angela could suddenly disappear.

And while Jake and I go searching for her, Traci can get set up with the camcorder," Brenda continued.

"I like it. I like the way you think," Traci said, grinning at Brenda. She turned to Angela. "I'll bring the camcorder over to your house the night before. We can hide it somewhere in the living room."

"Then, while Jake and I are searching for Angela, Angela climbs into the coffin and gets ready to scare Jake to death," Brenda said, thinking it through carefully.

"Then I guess Angela and I tie Jake up," she continued.

"I've got plenty of rope at home," Angela offered. "My parents always have several nooses hanging from the ceiling at Halloween time."

"Excellent!" Brenda said. She turned to Traci. "Do you think we should put Jake's head in a noose?"

"Why not?" Traci replied. "If one is handy, why not use it?"

"He'll have a cow! He really will!" Brenda declared.

"He deserves it," Traci said in a low voice. She changed to a grim expression and imitated Jake: *I don't like to be embarrassed.*

Brenda laughed. "I think he'll be embarrassed enough when we show everyone our videotape!"

"I just remembered — my parents have a really huge bullwhip in the closet," Angela said.

"Perfect! Get it!" Brenda urged. She couldn't keep the broad smile from spreading across her face. "This is going to be an interesting Halloween!"

After her friends left, Brenda loaded the plates into the dishwasher. She forced herself to stop thinking about Jake and the plan to pay him back.

I've got a ton of homework, she told herself. I've got to shove everything else out of my mind and start to concentrate on my work.

As she swept the pizza crumbs into her hand, Brenda heard noises. She stopped and listened.

Footsteps. From upstairs.

"Who's home?" she called.

No reply.

She tossed the crumbs into the sink and listened.

It couldn't be Randy, she knew. Randy was staying at a friend's until dinnertime.

Is Halley home? Brenda wondered.

She made her way to the front hall, pausing

at the bottom of the steps to listen.

Silence.

Holding on to the banister, she made her way quickly up the stairs.

The second-floor hallway was covered in darkness. Brenda clicked on the ceiling light — and gasped when she saw the tall figure standing against the wall.

"Dina — what are *you* doing here?" Brenda cried.

Chapter 19

Dressed in an oversized navy-blue sweater pulled down over black tights that made her long legs look even longer, Dina huddled against the wall and didn't reply.

"Dina — ?" Brenda choked out, frozen in place at the second-floor landing, staring in shock at this intruder.

Another figure stepped out of a bedroom doorway.

Halley.

"Oh, hi, Brenda," Halley said casually. "Dina and I were just going over our government notes." Halley had a strange smile on her lips, a pleased smile.

She knows that seeing Dina really freaked me out, Brenda realized. And she's happy about it.

Halley deliberately invited Dina here just to mess with my mind.

"What were you and your friends giggling about?" Halley asked, her smile fading to an expression of disapproval.

"Nothing much," Brenda replied.

"I'm just showing Dina out," Halley said.

"No need. I know the way," Dina said, avoiding Brenda's eyes.

Brenda stepped aside as Halley and Dina made their way past her to the stairs. How could Halley bring her into this house? Brenda wondered, feeling her anger grow. Halley knows that Dina tried to kill me last year.

I can't let Halley get away with this, Brenda decided.

She waited in the hall for her cousin to return. The front storm door slammed. She heard Halley's footsteps on the stairs.

"You're still here?" Halley asked coldly, glaring at Brenda.

"Why did you invite Dina here? Just to upset me?" Brenda demanded shrilly.

Halley stepped past her and made her way to her room. "I really think I'm allowed to have my own friends," she replied nastily.

Brenda followed her into the room. *"That's* who you choose for a friend? You know — "

"Dina is a really nice girl," Halley interrupted. She turned to face Brenda, pushing her piles of blond hair back over her shoulders.

"She *was* your best friend, after all. She went through a bad time. I think she deserves another chance. I — I really like her."

"You invited her here just to upset me!" Brenda cried.

"The world doesn't spin around you!" Halley shot back.

"You're just so obvious!" Brenda replied shrilly. "You'll do anything to hurt me. Anything!"

"You don't know what you're saying," Halley said through clenched teeth. "You never try to understand me. Never!" Tears formed in her eyes and slid down her flushed cheeks. She pulled out a bunch of tissues from the box on her dressertop.

"You only accuse me. You only think of yourself and *your* precious feelings! How do you think I feel, Brenda? Having a court decide that my parents are unfit, that I can't live with either of them anymore. Having to move in here with you — a cousin who *hates* me, who is so *jealous* of me?"

"Huh? Jealous?" Brenda shrieked. "Me — jealous of you? Halley, you are so conceited!"

"See?" Halley shot back triumphantly, as if having proven her point. "See? All you know is to call me names!"

About to explode, Brenda gritted her teeth,

tried to force back her anger. "You're the hateful one, Halley," she accused. "You're the one who sent me those hateful, threatening jacko'-lanterns. You're the one who stuffed the rotten thing in my locker and — "

"No!" Halley screamed. "No! No, I didn't! You see? Do you see how you always accuse me? I — I — " She let out a cry of rage.

Brenda took a step back. She had never seen Halley so furious, so totally out of control.

"Get out of my room!" Halley shrieked. "I know you think it's still your room — but it's *my* room now! Get out, Brenda! Get out — !"

"Okay, okay," Brenda said. She turned and hurried out into the hall. Feeling a jumble of emotions, she made her way to the stairway.

The walls seemed to tilt. The floor swayed under her feet.

She felt angry and upset and guilty and frightened — all at the same time.

Halley is a phony, she decided, her heart pounding as she started down the stairs. I don't believe her tears for a moment.

And I don't believe that she is innocent — that she didn't put that gross, rotted pumpkin in my locker.

She's a total phony. It was all an act. She thinks I'm dumb enough to fall for it.

Phony! Phony! Phony!

Or *is* she?

Brenda's thoughts rocked from side to side like a tiny boat on a stormy ocean.

Or have I been wrong about Halley all along? Have I accused her of something she didn't do?

Did she invite Dina over only because she liked her?

Brenda gripped the banister tightly. Her tossing emotions were making her dizzy.

Slowly, she made her way halfway down the stairs — and then stopped with a loud gasp.

The front door stood open.

Halley hadn't closed it after Dina left.

And through the glass storm door, Brenda saw a man lumbering up the front walk.

The red-faced fat man. The crazed man from the mall.

Chapter 20

What is he doing here?

How did he find me?

The sight of the man lumbering up onto the stoop, his face red, his expression menacing, froze Brenda on the stairs. Her knees buckled. She grabbed the banister tightly to keep from falling.

The door is wide open.

He's going to barge in.

He's going to kill us both.

Brenda knew she had to warn Halley. They had to get out of the house.

But there was no time.

And if she came the rest of the way down the stairs, the man would see her.

I'm trapped, she realized, feeling cold horror weigh down her body. *Totally trapped!*

The big man pushed up to the glass storm door. He shielded his eyes with one chubby pink hand. Then his tiny black eyes narrowed as he gazed into the front entryway.

He's going to walk right in, Brenda realized.

He's going to walk right in and see me frozen here on the staircase.

He knocked on the door. Hard. Hard enough to make the door frame rattle.

The sound jolted Brenda to life. She pulled herself back up the stairs. Her heart thudding in her chest, she dropped to her knees on the landing.

Why is he knocking?

He knows someone is home. He can see that the door is wide open.

Bending low, peering down the stairs, she could see him. He pulled his ragged overcoat around his shoulders. Then he knocked again, rattling the storm door frame.

Again, the sound sent shockwaves through Brenda's body.

The police!

She jumped to her feet. She lurched to her room. She grabbed the phone receiver with a trembling hand.

Pushing the emergency number, she listened hard.

Was that the storm door squeaking open?

Was the fat man in the house?

Was he climbing the stairs?

The phone rang once. A woman's voice said, "Police."

"Hurry!" Brenda cried breathlessly. "Please — hurry!" She managed to choke out her address.

The footsteps were right outside her door.

She uttered a terrified gasp.

"What is the nature of the problem?" the police woman asked.

"Just *hurry*!" Brenda shrieked.

Chapter 21

The receiver dropped from her hand as the footsteps stopped outside her bedroom door.

Brenda spun around to face the intruder.

"Halley!" she screamed.

"Is someone knocking downstairs?" Halley asked, leaning against the door frame.

"It — it's a man!" Brenda cried.

"What does he want?" Halley asked, fiddling with a strand of her hair.

"No — you don't understand!" Brenda pushed past her cousin and stepped out into the hallway. She held her breath and listened.

Silence.

"It's the maniac!" she whispered to Halley.

Halley's eyes revealed her surprise. "What?"

Brenda raised a finger to her lips. "Ssshhh." She listened again.

Silence.

Had he crept into the house? Was he prowling around downstairs? Would he be searching the upstairs next?

"I called the police," Brenda whispered.

"Let's get out of here!" Halley cried. She made her way to the stairs, taking long strides. Brenda followed close behind.

At the top of the stairway, Brenda lowered her head and stared down at the door.

No one there.

"He might be in the house," she whispered to Halley.

Halley reached the front entryway first. She peeked into the living room. Then she turned and shoved the storm door open with both hands, and burst outside.

Out into a gray, overcast afternoon. Into the chill air. Heavy clouds hovering low, threatening snow.

The cold air felt good on Brenda's burning cheeks as she darted out after her cousin. They ran down the middle of the yard, their sneakers sinking into the soft ground, and didn't turn to glance back at the house until they reached the street.

"Where is he?" Halley demanded breathlessly.

Brenda shrugged.

Halley narrowed her eyes at Brenda suspiciously. "Is this some kind of joke?"

"No way," Brenda told her, trembling all over. "He was here, Halley. The man they talked about in the news. He's following me. I don't know why. But he's here, and it's no joke."

Two police officers searched the house carefully. They found no sign of any intruder.

Brenda's parents arrived home while the search was underway. They found Brenda and Halley huddled in the driveway, too frightened to go back into the house. Brenda quickly explained what had happened.

The two officers appeared a few moments later, motioning for everyone to come in. "No one here," one of them reported as the other policeman scribbled in a small notepad. "He must have changed his mind and left."

The officer asked Brenda to start at the beginning. "When did you first see the man?" he asked as his partner continued to write. "Give me as full a description as you can."

Brenda told them about the evening at the mall, how she spotted him staring at her, how he chased Angela and her. She described the big man in detail. "His clothes are so shabby.

He looks like he might be a homeless man,"
she concluded. "And his expression — it's just
so scary, so angry."

"He fits the description," the officer with
the notepad said to his partner.

The first policeman nodded grimly. "This
might be the man we're looking for," he said
solemnly. "Keep your doors locked, okay? If
you see him again, just get away as fast as you
can. And call us. I don't want to scare you —
but this man could be very dangerous."

The other officer raised his eyes to Brenda.
"Do you have any idea why he's coming after
you?"

Brenda thought hard, chewing her lower lip.
"No idea," she murmured in reply. "No idea
at all."

Dinner was quiet. Randy had returned
home, and no one wanted to frighten him by
talking about the dangerous fat man.

Everyone tried to talk about other things.
But the conversation came out tense and
awkward.

Halley excused herself before dessert and
hurried up to her room. Mr. Morgan kept getting up to check the windows and make sure
they were locked.

After dinner, Randy insisted on demonstrating to Brenda a Nintendo game he had borrowed from a friend. Brenda tried to concentrate on the colorful, fighting images on the screen. But her mind kept drifting to other things.

Finally she escaped to her room and called Angela. "You must have been totally freaked!" Angela declared after Brenda told her all about the afternoon.

"I know I shouldn't blame her," Brenda told her friend. "But of course it was Halley who left the front door wide open."

"We have to include Halley in our little Halloween festivities," Angela suggested. "It would be great to get Jake and Halley at the same time, wouldn't it?"

"Yeah," Brenda agreed quickly. "But I don't see how we can get Halley over to your house. I mean, Halley would never agree to go trick-or-treating with us. Especially if she knew Jake was coming."

"I'll bet we could think of a way," Angela replied. "If we really put our minds to it." She snickered.

"Halley and Dina have become friends," Brenda revealed. "She invited Dina over here. I was so shocked — "

"That's horrible!" Angela cried. "That's just so mean. Halley's vicious, Bren. We have to include her in our Halloween party. We *have* to."

"First I have to get Jake to come," Brenda replied thoughtfully, shifting the phone to her other ear. "But that shouldn't be a problem."

She and Angela chatted a while longer, mainly about plans for scaring Jake on Halloween. After Brenda finally hung up the phone, she sat at her desk, staring out the window at the blue-black sky, thinking hard about Halley, trying to sort out her feelings.

Then she climbed to her feet and crossed the room to her bed. Maybe I'll slip into bed, get all warm and cozy, and read for a while, she thought.

That would be relaxing. And it would take my mind off everything else.

Escape. That's what I need right now.

She leaned over the bed and pulled down the heavy bedspread.

Her breath caught in her throat as the painted jack-o'-lantern came into view. It was painted in heavy orange and black, smeared over the pillowcase.

Frowning. Frowning up at her.

The frowning mouth was cut out of the pillowcase.

And inside the cut-out mouth — stretching

up from inside Brenda's pillow — were a dozen brown and purple worms, crawling and wriggling their way out of the jack-o'-lantern mouth, leaving slimy trails as they inched over the pillow and onto the bed.

Chapter 22

Brenda started to scream. But her anger quickly rose up over her horror.

Feeling the blood pulse at her temples, she spun away from the disgusting scene in the bed. The walls, the floor, the ceiling — all burned bright red from her anger.

She strode out of her room, burst down the hall, and pushed open Halley's bedroom door, shoving it so hard, it slammed against the wall.

Halley had changed into red-and-white-striped pajamas. She sat typing at her computer, her back to the door, the blue glow of the monitor falling over her.

Her head jerked around as the door slammed. Her eyes grew wide with surprise. "Brenda?"

Brenda lunged across the room.

Halley started to her feet — but she was too slow.

With a snarl of rage, Brenda grabbed Halley's hair with both hands — and pulled.

"The last straw!" Brenda shrieked in a shrill voice that seemed to come from deep inside her. "The last straw, Halley! The last straw!"

"Let *go* of me!" Halley cried. "Are you *crazy*!?"

Struggling to pull Halley off the desk chair, Brenda blinked — and blinked again. Everything glowed bright red. The computer monitor. The desk. Halley's hair. The whole room.

Red. Red as blood.

Red as Brenda's rage.

And now they were wrestling, wrestling on the red floor.

Pulling and hitting at each other, their arms thrashing, their legs kicking. Wrestling so desperately in the angry, swirling red.

"Let go! Let go!"

"How *could* you? How could you hate me so much?"

"Get *off* me!"

Like two wild animals, gasping and shrieking, struggling blindly, furiously.

Until Brenda felt strong arms pulling her away.

And her father's voice, close to her ear, insisting, "Get up, Brenda. Get up. Stop it now. Brenda, stop it — right now!"

The deep curtain of red slowly lifted.

Brenda saw that she was stretched over Halley, her knees on the carpet, her hands wrapped around Halley's wrists, pressing Halley's arms to the floor.

How did I get here?

What am I doing?

Have I totally lost it?

YES!

Her father gripped her roughly under the arms and tugged her up. "Brenda, what are you doing? What?"

"What's going on?" Randy's voice from the doorway.

Her temples pounding, Brenda shut her eyes, allowed herself to be dragged away, struggled to catch her breath, to stop her chest from heaving up and down, to stop the loud gasps that rose up from her throat.

"She attacked me!" Halley was screaming. "Like a wild animal! I'm not safe here! I'm not safe in my own house!"

"This is *my* house!" Brenda shrieked. "You can't fill it with worms! You can't!"

"Huh?" Halley climbed slowly to her feet, her hair falling over her face, the striped pajamas torn and twisted. "She's crazy! Brenda is totally crazy!"

* * *

Mr. and Mrs. Morgan forced Brenda to take deep breaths, to calm herself, before they followed her into her bedroom. Then they all trooped silently up to the bed.

"There! This is what Halley did!" Brenda declared, pulling back the covers to reveal the painted pumpkin, the crawling worms. "Still think she's so perfect? Still think *I'm* the crazy one?"

"Ooh, gross!" Randy declared, leaning close to get a good view. "Yuck!"

Brenda's parents stared in silent shock.

"I didn't do it!" Halley protested, shaking her head. "No way. Why do you say I did it, Brenda? Why do you think — ?"

"Who *else*?" Brenda screamed. "Who else? Who else?"

She felt her father's hands on her shoulders. "Sssshhh."

Halley shoved the hair off her face, then raised pleading eyes to Brenda's parents. "You don't think I did this, do you? You don't think I could do something like this?"

"Who else?" Brenda choked out, making no effort to get out from under her father's firm but gentle grasp on her shoulders.

"Who else was in the house today?" Mrs. Morgan asked softly.

"Don't look at me!" Randy declared. "I hate worms. They're too slimy!"

"Halley did it," Brenda said in a trembling voice. "It was Halley. It had to be Halley."

"Who else was here today?" Mrs. Morgan repeated, suddenly looking very tired.

"Dina was here," Brenda revealed. "Halley invited Dina here. They were both up here when I got home from school."

Mrs. Morgan's eyes grew wide with surprise. "Dina Smithers? Was here in the house?"

"Dina is okay now," Halley insisted heatedly. "Dina is my friend."

"Did Dina do this?" Mr. Morgan asked Halley, gesturing to the bed. "Tell the truth. Did she?"

Halley shook her head. "I was with Dina the whole time. She didn't go into Brenda's room. I swear."

"Liar! You're such a filthy liar!" Brenda cried. She felt her father squeeze her shoulders, a signal to stop.

"Who else was here?" Mrs. Morgan asked. "Anybody else?"

"Brenda's friends were here," Halley reported with a sneer. "One of them probably did it."

"Angela and Traci," Brenda murmured.

"We worked on our video. Downstairs." She raised her eyes to her mother. "They're my friends. They didn't do it."

"Did either of them come upstairs?" Mrs. Morgan demanded.

Brenda had to think. "Maybe. To use the bathroom. And to get some props from my room. But there's no way — "

"Well, Dina and I didn't do it!" Halley repeated angrily, examining her pajama shirt. Two buttons had been torn off.

"Look at that big, fat one!" Randy exclaimed, pointing to a worm on Brenda's pillow.

"Let's get the bed cleaned up," Brenda's father urged with a weary sigh. "So we can all get to sleep."

"But what about Halley?" Brenda demanded angrily.

"What about me?" Halley snapped, narrowing her eyes at Brenda.

"We have to have a long talk tomorrow," Mrs. Morgan said, frowning at Halley. "We have to get things settled between you two. We're all a family now. We have to act like a family."

"Randy — go downstairs and get a big garbage bag," Mr. Morgan ordered. "We have to throw out the pillow and the worms."

Randy obediently ran to get the garbage bag.

Shaking their heads, Brenda's parents started to pull the covers off the bed.

Brenda huddled against the wall. Halley stepped up beside her.

"You want trouble?" Halley whispered menacingly into Brenda's ear. "I haven't even started."

Chapter 23

That night, on fresh sheets and a new pillow, Brenda dreamed about the fat man. In the dream, he waited in Halley's room, sitting on the edge of Halley's bed, his shabby overcoat open, his eyes alert on the door to the hallway.

He's waiting there for me, Brenda realized as she dreamed. He's waiting in Halley's room for me to walk by.

She woke up trembling.

Her entire body tingled.

More worms?

Brenda sat up with a gasp.

No. No worms. She breathed a long sigh of relief.

Will I ever feel safe here again? she wondered sadly. Will I ever feel safe as long as Halley is around?

The next morning, she couldn't wait to get

to school, to get out of the house and away
from Halley.

It was a cold, clear October day. A frost
had covered the ground, making the front
lawns gleam like silver in the morning sunlight
as Brenda jogged to school.

Angela met her at her locker. "Everything
is ready," she announced, smiling.

"Ready? You mean at your house?" Brenda
asked, pulling off her backpack.

Angela nodded. Her dark eyes glowed with
excitement. "My house looks great. Really
terrifying. It's the perfect place to scare someone to death."

Brenda gave her a half-hearted smile. I'm
already half scared to death, she thought
unhappily. Maybe our plan isn't such a hot
idea.

But then, glancing over at Angela, Brenda
saw Jake down the hall. He had his arms
draped casually over the shoulders of two
ninth-grade girls. He was walking between
them, coming on to both of them at the same
time.

Jake is asking for it, Brenda thought angrily.
He's been asking for it for a long time.

She turned to Angela. "I can't wait for Halloween," she said, her eyes on Jake. "I really
can't."

* * *

"The skeleton costumes are great," Brenda told Traci, cradling the cordless phone between her chin and shoulder. "Where did you find them?"

"At that party store on Madison Road," Traci replied. She had to shout over the roar of the vacuum cleaner in the background. "Why does my mom always like to vacuum at night?" she asked Brenda. "That's so weird."

"I tried my costume on," Brenda continued, glancing at the black-and-white costume draped over her desk chair. "It looks really creepy."

"The guy at the store thought I was crazy," Traci replied. "I bought the last four skeleton costumes he had. But I just thought it would be even creepier if we all dressed alike."

The vacuum cleaner roar ended abruptly. "Thank goodness!" Traci declared. "So do you think Jake will wear the skeleton costume? Did you talk to him, Bren?"

"Yeah. Everything is cool," Brenda replied, pacing her bedroom as she talked into the cordless phone. "I talked to Jake. He's definitely going trick-or-treating with you and me. At first, he thought it was a babyish idea. But then he said why should little kids have all the fun?"

"And he agreed to dress like us in a skeleton costume?"

"He's picking up the costume after school tomorrow," Brenda replied. "He didn't have a costume. So he was glad we got him one."

"This is going to be awesome!" Traci exclaimed. "I can't wait to make Jake squirm. I have the camcorder batteries all powered up and ready to go."

"Angela is sure excited," Brenda commented. She dropped down onto the edge of her bed. She could hear music playing in Halley's room next door. Thinking about Halley made her shudder.

"I guess Angela's parents did a great job with the eerie decorations," Traci said. "Did Angela say her parents would be home?"

"She didn't say," Brenda replied distractedly, thinking about Halley. She leaned back against the headboard. "Let's go over the plan one more time, Traci. I just want to get it clear in my mind."

"For sure," Traci replied. "You and I and Jake go trick-or-treating in our skeleton costumes. We end up at Angela's house."

"Check," Brenda said, trying to concentrate. The music from Halley's room had been turned up. Was Halley deliberately trying to annoy her?

It was a safe bet.

"Angela's front door is open," Traci continued. "The three of us go inside. 'Where is Angela?' one of us asks. We lead Jake to the coffins in the living room. Angela is inside one of the coffins. Her arm hangs out of it, just like the time we visited."

"Right," Brenda remembered. "And you and I let Jake be the one to discover Angela. 'Oh no! She's dead!' one of us cries."

"Right. This is so cool!" Traci exclaimed into the phone. "Then I pick up the camcorder and start taping Jake's terrified reaction. Angela slowly comes alive. We grab Jake. We tie him up. Then we really scare him. We make him think he's really in danger. We make him beg us to let him go. We make him plead and grovel. And I tape the whole thing."

Brenda snickered. "It's really sick," she admitted. "But it's great. Jake deserves it. He really does."

"He shouldn't have wrecked our first video," Traci replied. "But in a way, I'm glad he did. Because this new video is going to be even scarier!"

Both girls laughed.

"Think we'll really scare Jake?" Brenda asked.

"We'll scare him to death!" Traci exclaimed gleefully.

Chapter 24

"We're twins!" Jake declared from behind the plastic skull mask.

Brenda stuck out both bony arms. "Ta-daa! Instant diet!" She did a short skeleton dance. The black-and-white costume made a scratchy sound with every move she made.

"Cool," Jake said. "This is definitely way cool."

They were standing in Brenda's living room, admiring each other's costumes. Jake had pulled the skeleton top down over his sweatshirt. But the costume pants had been too small for him. His black denim jeans matched nicely, though.

He had been half an hour late, as usual.

"Sorry. I got hung up," he said. His usual thoughtless explanation.

"We'd better hurry. Traci is waiting for us," Brenda told him, starting for the door.

Jake blocked her way. He pulled up her mask. Then he slid his mask up on his head and smiled at her. "This was a cool idea," he said. He leaned forward and kissed her.

You have no idea *how* cool! Brenda thought, returning the kiss.

Last year was a Halloween I'd like to forget, she told herself. But this is definitely one I'll want to remember.

She pulled her mask down. "Come on. Let's go. This is going to be so much fun!"

She handed him a small shopping bag for collecting trick-or-treat candy. Then they stepped out into a crisp, clear night. An orange full moon, round as a pumpkin, hovered low over the bare trees.

Brenda's breath steamed up from the open mouth of the skeleton mask. She jogged down the driveway, eager to get to Traci's house, eager to get the real fun under way.

"Too bad the bones don't glow in the dark," Jake said, trotting alongside her. "Then we could really scare some little kids."

Don't worry, Jake, Brenda thought gleefully, *there will be plenty of scares tonight!*

Jake took her hand as Traci's house came into view. "Glad I decided to give you another chance?" he asked.

The question made Brenda stop. She spun

around to face him, staring through the eye-holes in the white skull mask. "What did you say?"

"I asked if you were glad I decided to give you another chance. I mean, you seemed pretty upset before. When I started seeing Halley. So, I thought I'd give you another shot." He laughed.

What a pig! Brenda thought angrily.

How can anyone be so totally stuck-up?

"Hey — there's Traci!" she cried, pointing. "Traci! Hi!"

Traci stood in a square of light on her front stoop. She was tucking her straight black hair inside the black skeleton hood. When she saw Brenda and Jake, she waved and started down the driveway.

"This is great!" Traci exclaimed breathlessly. "It's like being a kid again. Let's stop at every house." She waved her trick-or-treat bag. "I want a year's supply of candy!"

Jake laughed. "That'll make my dad real happy," he declared. Jake's dad was a dentist.

Traci and Brenda exchanged glances. Brenda could see the excitement in Traci's dark eyes. She's really pumped for this, like me! Brenda thought. Wait till I tell Traci what Jake the Pig just said to me. She'll howl!

At the first house, a middle-aged man and

woman came to the door. "Three skeletons!" the man declared. "Did you three copy each other?"

"No. Just a coincidence," Brenda joked.

The man and woman both snickered. "Very original," the woman said. She dropped tiny Tootsie Rolls into their bags.

The second house was completely dark. No one answered the door.

At the next house, a woman answered with two small girls, about three or four years old, who huddled close to her. "Look at the funny skeletons!" the woman declared. But her daughters hid behind her.

"We're not scary! Really!" Traci insisted to the little girls.

One of them opened one eye and peeked out at them.

"BOO!" Jake shouted.

Both little girls cried out and pressed tighter against their mother.

The woman rolled her eyes. "Thanks a bunch," she said sarcastically. She dropped miniature Milky Ways into the bags, then quickly closed the door.

"Jake, you really scared those little girls," Brenda scolded him as they cut over the front yard to the next house.

"They'll get over it," he replied, adjusting his mask.

A sharp wind made the light fabric of the costumes flutter. Brenda felt a chill run down her back. I should have worn another layer under this thing, she thought. She had on two T-shirts and a sweater, but she already felt cold.

Across the street, two ghosts and a witch, accompanied by a man in a heavy overcoat, probably their father, appeared in the light of a streetlamp. The father stood watch on the sidewalk as the ghosts and witch scurried up to the front porch.

Brenda led the way to the next house. A gruff-looking man in a blue work uniform pulled open the door. He narrowed his eyes at the three teenagers. "Aren't you kids a little old for trick-or-treat?" he rasped.

"We're big for our age!" Jake cracked.

The man laughed. He dropped a green apple into each bag. His smile faded. "I don't care how big you are," he said in a low voice. "Better be careful tonight. You know, that nut is still out there somewhere. They were just talking about him on the news."

Brenda sighed to herself as she led the way down the driveway. Why did he have to remind us of that creep? she asked herself. I was having so much fun, acting like a kid, not thinking about the fat man or about Halley or anything.

Black wisps of cloud snaked over the moon. The wind cut sharply, making their costumes flap. Somewhere down the block, a metal garbage can tipped over, sending the lid clattering down the driveway.

As they made their way across the street, Jake reached into his bag. He pulled out the green apple and heaved it as hard as he could down the sidewalk. "I hate green apples," he muttered. "Why do people give apples instead of candy on Halloween? It's sick. It really is."

Brenda laughed at him. "You're still a ten-year-old," she accused.

He growled at her. "Give me a break."

They continued trick-or-treating for another half hour. Their bags were about a third full by the time they passed a dark wooded lot, and Angela's house loomed into view.

"Hey, there's Angela's," Traci said casually. "She said we should stop by. She said she'd have some warm cider for us."

"Great!" Brenda replied. "I can use it. I'm freezing!"

"Angela lives in that weird old house?" Jake asked, staring up at the twin stone turrets.

"Yeah. That's her house," Brenda told him. "It's kind of creepy outside, but it's nice inside," she lied, glancing at Traci. She could tell that Traci was grinning under her mask.

Their sneakers crunching loudly, they started up the gravel driveway, making their way past the overgrown, weed-choked front lawn.

The porch light was on, casting a triangle of orange light down over the front stoop.

As they neared the house, Brenda hesitated.

She stopped as the object on the stoop came into clear focus.

"I don't believe it!" Brenda gasped.

Chapter 25

The big pumpkin on the porch had been carved into a jack-o'-lantern.

A frowning jack-o'-lantern.

As Brenda moved toward it, her hands raised to the cheeks of her mask, its angry, glowing triangular eyes stared back at her.

And she saw that the jack-o'-lantern rested on a wide puddle of red.

Just like the card she had received.

Happy Last Halloween.

The words flashed into Brenda's mind.

Why did Angela do that? she asked herself. She quickly answered the question herself: Because this was the scariest looking jack-o'-lantern Angela could think of.

And everything had to be as scary as possible tonight.

For Jake's sake.

"Cool jack-o'-lantern," Jake muttered as

they stepped onto the stoop. "Looks like Mr. McCurdy."

Mr. McCurdy was the assistant principal at McKinley High.

Brenda pushed the doorbell, then stepped back. She waited a while, then pressed it again.

"Hey, Angela!" Traci called in. She turned to Brenda. "Where is she?"

Brenda and Traci exchanged glances.

"You sure she's home?" Jake asked impatiently.

Brenda pointed. "The front door — it's open a little."

"Let's go in," Traci suggested, shivering. "She said she'd be waiting for us."

Brenda held the storm door open. Jake pushed the front door. It swung open, creaking loudly.

They stepped into the entryway. "Hey — Angela?" Traci called.

The narrow entryway was dark except for the flickering orange light from a candle on a low table. In the quivering light, Brenda could see sheets of cobwebs over the doorway.

Somber organ music floated from the living room. Funeral music, Brenda thought. Low and mournful.

"Angela?" Traci called again. "Is anyone home?"

"Wow," Jake muttered, glancing up at the shadowy spiderwebs. "Awesome decorations! She really gets into Halloween — doesn't she?" He took a step into the doorway to the living room and stopped.

"Oh, man!" He slid the mask up onto his head to see better.

Brenda and Traci crept up behind him.

Lighted by a tall candelabra on the mantelpiece, the living room stretched out in eerie splendor. Curtains of filmy cobwebs caught the darting candlelight. The two black coffins glowed darkly in the center of the bare room.

Heavy, dark drapes covered the big front window. Against the wall across from the window, three more frowning jack-o'-lanterns, glowing brightly, were lined up on the floor. Each jack-o'-lantern had a knife — a big, black-handled kitchen knife — shoved into its side.

Oh, sick! Brenda thought. Angela's parents really have twisted imaginations!

"I don't *believe* this!" Jack exclaimed quietly, his eyes moving around the room.

"I just don't understand why Angela isn't here," Traci repeated, sounding worried.

Traci is a good actress, Brenda thought. She

almost has *me* believing that she's upset about Angela.

"Look at that!" Jake cried, pointing across the room to the den.

The two skeletons sat side by side in the doorway, gray-green in the dim light, leaning against each other, grinning into the dark living room.

"They look real!" Jake exclaimed. "This is so great!" He dropped his trick-or-treat bag to the floor and made his way over to the coffins.

Brenda stared down at the three frowning jack-o'-lanterns with the big knives plunged into their sides. A loud burst of organ music made her jump.

"Where do you think Angela's parents got these coffins?" Traci asked, motioning for Brenda to step up beside them.

Brenda moved forward, lowering her eyes to the coffin on the right, expecting to see Angela's pale arm hanging from under the lid.

To her surprise, the coffin lid was tightly closed.

No sign of Angela.

Brenda turned to the coffin on the left. The lid on this coffin was also closed. The flickering light from the candelabra was reflected darkly on its polished surface.

What's up with Angela? Brenda wondered. She slid the white skull mask up onto her forehead and stared at the closed coffins.

Angela is supposed to be hiding in that one with her arm hanging out, she thought. What is Angela trying to do?

Did she change the plan at the last minute?

"Angela? Angela? Anybody home?" Traci shouted.

Jake ran his hand over the smooth wood of one of the coffins. "I've never been this close to a real coffin before," he said. "This is really awesome!"

Is Angela inside, waiting for us to pull open the lid? Brenda wondered.

Did she decide at the last minute that would be scarier?

Can she breathe in there with the lid shut so tight?

The low, mournful notes of the organ music rose over the room. A sharp wind gust made the windowpanes rattle behind the dark drapes.

The candles on the mantel dipped low in an unseen breeze.

Angela, are you waiting in there for us? Brenda wondered, feeling her heart start to race.

Are you waiting inside the coffin to terrify

Jake? Are you waiting for us to pick up the lid?

"Let's see what's inside the coffin," Jake suggested, grinning at Brenda. "Help me push up the lid, okay?"

Brenda obediently stepped forward to help. Out of the corner of her eye, she saw Traci bend to pick up the camcorder, which had been hidden on the floor behind the other coffin.

"Think there's anything in here?" Jake asked.

"I — I don't know," Brenda stammered, trying to make herself sound frightened.

Get ready, Jake, she thought eagerly.

Get ready for the scare of your life.

The two of them pushed at the heavy coffin lid.

Slowly, slowly, it slid up.

Her arms still braced against it, Brenda peered into the dark coffin — and uttered a low cry.

Chapter 26

The coffin was empty.

"It's all shiny inside," Jake said, running his hand over the padded satin. "Looks comfy, doesn't it?" He grinned at Brenda.

But Brenda didn't return his smile.

Something is wrong, she thought, feeling a knot of dread tighten her stomach. Angela is supposed to be in here.

"Let's check out the other coffin," she suggested.

As she turned, she caught a glimpse of Traci, standing back in the shadows, the camcorder raised to her eye. There won't be much to tape, Brenda thought wistfully, if Angela doesn't follow the plan.

She and Jake pushed up the lid of the other coffin. This one was empty, too. A sour, musty odor floated up from the cushioned coffin bottom.

154

The smell of death, Brenda thought grimly.

Where *is* Angela?

Jake grabbed her hand. "Let's get in," he whispered, bringing his mouth close to her ear. "You and me. Just to see what it feels like."

Brenda pulled away from him. She forced a laugh. "That's the *worst* invitation I've had all year!" she joked.

"Come on, Bren — " Jake urged. "Let's try it out."

Ignoring him, Brenda turned to Traci, who had lowered the camcorder to the windowsill. "We've got to find Angela," Brenda said. "I don't understand why she isn't here."

"Maybe she went trick-or-treating," Jake suggested, lowering the coffin lid.

"No. She said she'd wait for us," Traci replied.

"Let's look for her," Brenda urged, searching the shadow-filled room once again. Her eyes landed on the two skeletons, leaning together, their bones reflecting the darting candlelight.

"Angela! Angela!" Traci shouted, cupping her hands around her mouth.

No reply. The dreary organ music droned on.

"I'll try the kitchen and the back of the

house," Brenda said, her voice catching. The feeling of dread was tightening her throat. "You try upstairs," she told Traci.

Jake started to the den. "I'll ask those two skeletons if they've seen her," he joked.

This isn't a joke, Brenda thought as she made her way to the kitchen. Everything is ready according to our plan. The front door was left open. The eerie music is playing. The jack-o'-lanterns are all lighted.

So where is Angela?

The big kitchen lay in darkness. Brenda fumbled for the light switch, found it, clicked it on. Fluorescent lights flickered on in the ceiling.

"Angela?" Brenda called meekly.

No sign of her.

Brenda's eyes surveyed the kitchen. Neat and clean. Everything in its place.

She turned and started into the back hall. "Angela?" she called again.

No reply.

A small round ceiling fixture cast pale white light over the threadbare carpet. Walking slowly through the unfamiliar hallway, she passed a small pantry, a supply closet, an empty room.

She was nearly to the end of the hall when a dark figure stepped out of a doorway.

"Oh!" Brenda cried out in surprise. "Angela? Where *were* you?"

The figure stepped into the light. She wore a witch's costume, a pointed hat, a long, shiny black skirt, a black blouse, a black mask over her eyes.

Brenda saw at once that it wasn't Angela.

Brown eyes stared at Brenda through the eyeholes of the mask.

"Who — who *are* you?" Brenda managed to stammer.

Slowly, the witch raised one hand and lifted off the mask.

Brenda gasped.

"Dina!" she cried. "What are *you* doing here?"

Chapter 27

"Angela invited me," Dina replied, rolling the mask between her fingers.

"She *what*?" Brenda couldn't hide her shock.

"She called Halley and me," Dina continued. "She invited us over. She said she was having a Halloween party, and everyone from our class would be here. But — "

"Halley is here, too?" Brenda demanded shrilly.

As if on cue, Halley appeared at the end of the hallway. She was dressed in her normal clothes — a navy-blue turtleneck sweater and faded denim jeans. But she carried a rubber gorilla mask in her hand. "Where is your friend Angela?" she asked Brenda.

"I — I'm looking for her, too," Brenda stammered. "I didn't expect to see you — "

"We just got here," Dina explained, glancing at Halley. "But we can't find Angela.

Where *is* everyone? Where's the party?"

"Is this some kind of stupid prank?" Halley demanded sharply.

"No!" Brenda insisted. "I mean . . . I don't know. Angela was supposed to be here. I don't understand. I didn't think she was inviting anyone. Traci, and Jake, and me — we were — "

"Is *Jake* here?" Halley demanded. She grabbed Dina's arm. "Let's get out of here."

"Whoa. Cool your jets," Dina replied, her dark eyes flaring. "I want to find Angela. If this is all a joke, I want to tell her what I think of it."

"No way!" Halley cried. "No way I want to see that creep Jake. Let's just get out of here, and — "

A loud cry from the front of the house made Halley stop.

"It's Traci!" Brenda exclaimed. "Maybe she found Angela."

Brenda turned and began running toward the living room. She could hear Halley and Dina a few steps behind her.

They burst into the darkness of the living room to find Traci standing by herself in front of the coffins. "Traci, did you find her?" Brenda demanded breathlessly.

Traci's mouth dropped open, but no sound came out.

She pointed with a trembling finger to the coffin on the left.

"Traci — what's wrong?" Brenda asked, hurrying over to her.

She saw at once what had frightened Traci.

A hand hung limply from inside the coffin on the left.

"Is it Angela?" Brenda cried. She squinted at the hand, poking out from under the dark lid. In the flickering orange candlelight, it was impossible to see.

Traci raised both hands to her face. She still hadn't uttered a sound.

"What's going on?" Brenda heard Halley demand from the entryway. "The house is decorated for a party. So where's the party?"

Ignoring her cousin, Brenda moved forward quickly. She gripped the smooth coffin lid with both hands and pushed up.

It lifted slowly.

When the lid stood upright, Brenda jumped back — and stared inside.

"Jake!" she cried.

His eyes bulged lifelessly, blankly. His mouth gaped open, twisted in an expression of ugly horror.

"Jake! No!"

A black-handled kitchen knife had been plunged into his chest. Bright red blood flowed in a circle onto the white rib bones of the skeleton costume.

Brenda grabbed his hand. Still warm. But soft as a sponge.

"He — he's dead," she murmured.

Chapter 28

Brenda staggered back.

She couldn't remove her eyes from the dark circle of blood spreading over Jake's costumed chest.

She could hear Halley and Dina screaming shrilly behind her. She could hear Traci moaning and repeating Jake's name.

She staggered back until she hit the wall. Lowering her eyes, she saw that the knife was missing from one of the three frowning jack-o'-lanterns.

Someone had pulled it from the jack-o'-lantern and plunged it into Jake's chest.

Someone. Someone.

"Call the police! Quick!" Halley was shrieking. "Somebody — call!"

Brenda blinked several times, trying to make the shadows stop dancing, trying to make the room stop tilting.

If only there was some light in the room. If only the horrid organ music would stop. If only . . .

She glanced across the room to see Dina bending low.

To pick up another knife?

To murder someone else in the room?

The questions flickered in Brenda's mind like the candlelight from the mantel. Dark, shadowy questions filled with fear.

Forcing herself away from the wall, Brenda moved quickly to stop Dina — then stopped as she realized Dina was reaching for the phone.

Dina frantically punched the buttons, pressing the receiver to her ear. A second later, she uttered a low cry, and the phone receiver fell from her hand.

"The phone — it's dead," Dina murmured. "Completely dead."

"Let's get to the neighbors!" Halley suggested, breathing hard.

"There *are* no neighbors!" Brenda told her. "Only woods."

"Then let's get *out* of here!" Halley screamed.

A loud *thump* above their heads made them all freeze.

The sound repeated, a heavy bump. On the ceiling.

"Let's go!" Halley urged frantically. "There's a killer — !"

"Wait!" Brenda raised a hand to stop them.

Another heavy *thud* above their heads.

"Wait!" Brenda repeated. "That might be Angela up there. She may be trying to signal us, trying to get our help."

"Let's go!" Halley started to the front door.

"We can't just leave Angela here!" Brenda screamed.

Without waiting for a reply, she made her way to the stairway. Then, her heart pounding, she pulled herself up the stairs.

The banging sound grew louder as Brenda reached the second-floor landing. She followed it down the dark hall, pushed open a half-closed door, and stepped into a bedroom.

Angela's bedroom.

The bed made. The dressertop tidy. Lipstick tubes and makeup neatly arranged.

A loud *thud* to Brenda's left.

She turned, struggling to breathe against the terror that choked her throat.

The closet door was shut tight.

The banging came from the closet.

Brenda reached for the doorknob with a

trembling hand. Grasped it. Pulled open the closet door.

"Angela!"

Inside the dark closet, Angela, in her skeleton costume, sat crouched in a wooden chair, struggling against the ropes that held her. A plaid kerchief had been tied tightly around her lower face, gagging her.

"Angela! You're here!" Brenda cried breathlessly. She tugged the kerchief away. "What happened? Who — ?"

Angela swallowed hard. She took a deep breath. Then another.

"Angela — what happened?" Brenda repeated, bending to untie the rope that held Angela to the chair. The knot was loose. It slipped away easily.

"It's the maniac!" Angela managed to cry, her voice a harsh whisper. "The fat man! The maniac, Brenda! He — he tied me up! And — he's still here! He says he's going to kill us all! He's still here, Brenda! He's still in the house!"

Chapter 29

Brenda bent to help Angela to her feet. "Jake's dead!" Brenda blurted out. "Jake's already dead!"

"No!" Angela uttered. She grabbed the side of the closet to keep from falling. "I don't believe it."

"Come on," Brenda urged. "We have to get out of here!"

She helped Angela down the stairs. The others waited in the front entryway. Traci had her hands covering her face. Her trembling shoulders revealed that she was crying.

Dina and Halley huddled by the door.

"It's the fat man!" Brenda cried. "He's *here*!"

The news was greeted with shrieks and cries of fear.

Moving unsteadily, her arms out in front of her, Angela lunged into the living room. She bent quickly and pulled a big kitchen knife from the nearest jack-o'-lantern. "For protection," she explained. "I — I'm so frightened. He tied me up. He was coming back for me. Let's go — please!"

They had all followed Angela into the living room. Now they moved again to the front door.

"Wait!" Traci cried suddenly, startling everyone. Traci's cheeks were red and puffy. She wiped tears away with both hands. "The camcorder!" she cried.

"Just leave it," Brenda told her.

"No. You don't understand," Traci replied in a trembling voice. "I left it on. The whole time. The murderer must be on the tape. It's aimed at the coffin — don't you see? The whole thing is on the tape!"

Traci darted into the living room to grab the camcorder from the windowsill. Brenda and the others waited in the entryway to the living room.

When Brenda turned back to the front door, she found Angela blocking the way, the wide-bladed knife raised above her waist.

"If it's all on tape," Angela said softly, her dark eyes moving from one girl to another. "If it's all on tape, I have no choice. I have to kill you all."

Chapter 30

"Angela — are you *crazy*?" Brenda shrieked. "Open the door. Let us out!"

With a quick motion, Angela bolted the front door shut. "Get back! Get into the living room!" she instructed, her dark eyes flaring angrily.

With a desperate cry, Brenda grabbed for the knife.

Angela swung it hard. The blade swiped past Brenda's face, missing her by less than an inch.

Gasping, Brenda sank back.

"I'm serious," Angela told them all, her voice a menacing whisper. "Get in the living room — now."

Brenda obediently led the way into the dark living room. Her eyes fell on the open coffin, on Jake's lifeless body sprawled inside, one hand hanging limply over the side.

She forced herself to look away. "Angela — you — you killed Jake?"

Angela nodded coolly, her face expressionless. "Yes. And then I ran upstairs and tied myself up in the closet. But I didn't count on the camcorder being on."

"It wasn't," Traci revealed in a soft voice just above a whisper. "It wasn't on. I just said that. I thought maybe it would force the murderer to reveal herself."

"Clever, Traci," Angela said, sneering. "Very clever. But, who cares?" She waved the big knife.

"You — did everything, didn't you," Brenda accused weakly. "The frowning jack-o'-lantern, the rotted pumpkin, the worms . . ." Her voice cracked.

Angela nodded, a grim smile playing over her lips. "It was so easy, Bren," she replied. "I could do whatever I wanted. There was no way you wouldn't trust poor, chubby Angela. The new girl. The lonely new girl."

"I should have known," Brenda murmured. "You were so eager to set this all up. So eager . . ."

"Yes. You should have known," Angela repeated bitterly.

"But, Angela — " Brenda protested. "I was

your friend. I was always a real friend."

Angela shook her head. "Some friend," she muttered darkly. "Is that why you stole Jake from me?"

"Huh?" Traci gasped. "Brenda didn't steal Jake — !"

"Shut up!" Angela screamed nastily. "Jake said he *wanted* to go out with me after he dumped Brenda. But Brenda wouldn't let him. Brenda wouldn't let him go, so — "

"You're crazy!" Brenda blurted out. "That's not true at all, Angela! You're crazy!"

Angela's features tightened in fury. She narrowed her eyes menacingly at Brenda. "Don't say I'm crazy. Don't say I'm crazy in front of my parents!"

"Huh?" Brenda let out a startled gasp.

"Where are your parents, Angela?" she heard Halley ask. "Where are they?"

"Don't say I'm crazy in front of my parents," Angela repeated angrily. She pointed across the room to the two skeletons. "Mommy and Daddy are listening."

Brenda swallowed hard as she stared at the grinning skeletons, leaning against each other in the folding chairs. She suddenly felt sick. She struggled against the waves of nausea that choked her.

"Angela, those aren't your parents," Halley

said softly. "Where are your parents?"

Angela raised the knife. "Those *are* my parents!" she insisted. "The only parents I have!"

Oh, she's so sick, Brenda thought, feeling a chill of terror. *She's so terribly sick.*

"Why shouldn't I have my mommy and daddy with me?" Angela demanded, raising her voice. "Why shouldn't I have parents like everyone else?"

"Angela, please — " Traci started.

"Why shouldn't I have a family?" Angela shouted, completely losing control. "And why shouldn't I have a boyfriend like everyone else? Jake promised me! He promised we'd go out! But he lied — and so he had to die!"

She moved quickly toward Brenda, hatred flaring in her eyes. "All your fault, Brenda!" Angela screamed. "All your fault! So it's your turn next!"

Brenda raised her hands as if to shield herself. She tried to dodge out of Angela's path.

But Angela moved too quickly.

Brenda opened her mouth to scream as the knife blade swung down toward her chest.

Chapter 31

A flash of yellow light.

Brenda waited for the pain to shoot through her body.

But the knife blade stopped inches above her.

And as Brenda staggered back, she saw what caused the bright swirl of light, saw clearly in such sharp focus, clearly and slowly, as if it were happening in slow motion.

She saw Halley raise the glowing jack-o'-lantern — and slam it hard over Angela's head.

The pumpkin bobbed on Angela's shoulders. The triangular eyes continued to glow orange for a moment.

The frowning jack-o'-lantern replaced Angela's angry face.

Then the pumpkin eyes dimmed as the candle inside died.

Angela's hands thrashed the air wildly. And from inside the pumpkin, her screams shattered the heavy silence.

"It's *scalding* me! Ohhhh! It's *buuuurrning* me!"

Angela dropped to her knees, both hands clawing at the pumpkin, tearing helplessly, her screams of agony rising over the droning of the funereal organ music.

As Brenda stared in horror, she suddenly felt a comforting arm slide around her shoulders. "Brenda, are you okay? Did she hurt you? Are you okay?"

Halley held her tightly, her features tight with worry. "That was so close . . . so close," Halley whispered.

Halley cares about me, Brenda suddenly knew.

And I care about her, too.

Brenda realized she had a lot of apologizing to do. "You saved my life, Halley," she managed to choke out.

She turned to see Traci and Dina holding Angela down. The jack-o'-lantern had been pulled away. Pumpkin seeds clung to Angela's curly hair. Angela, hunched on her knees, sobbed, covering her burned face with both hands.

"We'll be right back," Brenda said. Then she and Halley hurried to call the police.

The next day, Brenda slept till the afternoon. The horror of the night before lingered as she stretched and slowly climbed out of bed.

The police and their questions rolled through her mind. Hours of questions. And then the horrible moment when Jake's parents were called.

And then all of the parents were there. And there were tears and hugs and hours more of explanations.

And how could anyone explain? How could anyone explain what had been in Angela's mind? What had made her live alone in that creepy house with coffins for furniture? What had made her think the plastic skeletons were her parents?

What had made her kill?

Will I ever be able to forget all of this? Brenda wondered as she dressed and brushed her hair. Will I ever have normal thoughts again? Can I ever leave the horror of Halloween night behind?

Feeling shaky and drained, she made her way downstairs to the kitchen. Halley must have slept late, too, Brenda saw. She was at the kitchen table, still in pajamas, eating breakfast.

Brenda started into the kitchen — but stopped short when she heard a sharp knock on the front door. Spinning around, she saw that the door was open.

"Oh, no!" Brenda uttered.

Through the glass storm door, she stared at the fat man, peering back at her, his face red, his dark eyes angry, his fist pounding the glass.

Chapter 32

He's seen me, Brenda realized.

I'm trapped. I can't run.

The man stared in, face pressed to the glass, his fist pounding the storm door.

"Dad! Mom!" Brenda called.

Her father appeared behind her. "He — he's here!" Brenda cried.

Mr. Morgan's features were set in a hard stare. He strode past Brenda, through the hall, and pushed open the storm door. "Can I help you?" he demanded sternly.

"Is that your daughter?" the man pointed in at Brenda, who huddled against the staircase wall.

"Yes," Brenda's father replied curtly.

"Well, this belongs to her," the man said. He held up Brenda's brown leather wallet.

"I've been trying to return this for days," the man said, sighing.

"Huh?" A shocked cry escaped Brenda's lips.

Her father opened the glass door. The man lumbered into the entryway, carefully wiping his tattered shoes on the floor mat. He handed the wallet to Brenda.

"I saw it fall out of your bag. At the mall. I picked it up and chased after you. But you wouldn't listen to me. So I found the address in your wallet. But — "

"Sorry," Brenda said, feeling her cheeks grow hot. "I shouldn't have run. I just thought . . ." Her voice trailed off.

The man turned to Mr. Morgan. "I . . . I wouldn't have bothered," he said quietly, "but I'm a little down on my luck. I thought there might be . . . uh . . . a reward." He lowered his eyes.

Mr. Morgan thanked the man again and handed him a ten-dollar bill.

A few seconds later, the man was gone. Brenda sat across from Halley at the kitchen table, rolling the wallet around in her hands.

She gazed up at her cousin and shook her head. "What a nightmare. Halloween is defi-

nitely not my favorite time of year," she said,
sighing.

Halley reached across the table to pat Brenda's hand. "Next Halloween," she suggested,
"let's pretend it's Thanksgiving. *Everybody*
loves Thanksgiving!"

About the Author

R.L. STINE is the author of more than three dozen mysteries for young people, all of which have been best-sellers. Recent Scholastic horror titles include *Call Waiting*, *The Baby-sitter III*, *The Dead Girlfriend*, and *Halloween Night*.

In addition, he is the author of two popular monthly series: *Goosebumps* and *Fear Street*.

Bob lives in New York City with his wife, Jane, and fourteen-year-old son, Matt.

THRILLERS

P•INT CRiME

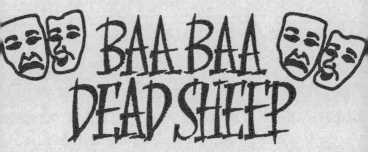

BAA BAA DEAD SHEEP

Everyone hated Mr. Lamb, the creepy caretaker of the Tree Theatre. Then someone decided to teach him a lesson. It was supposed to be a little prank...but someone brought Mr. Lamb to the slaughter.

Don't miss these gripping Point Crime mysteries available wherever you buy books, or use order form below.

❑	BAU 48320-X	**Formula for Murder**	$3.50
❑	BAU 48318-8	**Deadly Secrets**	$3.50
❑	BAU 48319-6	**School for Terror**	$3.50